Generations
Life's Journeys

"Lock up your libraries if you like; but there is no gate, no lock, no bolt that you can set upon the freedom of my mind."
— *Virginia Woolf, A Room of One's Own*

Acknowledgements

The Write-On Writer's Workshop wish to thank the following:

The West Oakland Senior Center Advisory Board
(financial support)

Dorothy L. Poston and WOSC Staff
(space, printing and refreshments)

Jean Mundy (proof-reading and editing)

Jennifer D. King (introduction)

Mary Cathy Tate (lead moderator)

Douglas E. Coleman (assistant lead moderator)

Workshop Participants:
Mary Cathy Tate, Douglas E. Coleman, Lucy Ely,
Jennifer D. King, Juliana Whitten, Willie Francis, Dorothy L. Poston,
Clotile Sanford Hunt, Betty L. Walker and Doris Phelps

I

II

About Our Founder

Jan Faulkner created the Chester Himes Black Mystery Writers Conference in Oakland, which brought together famous and not-famous authors, writers, and readers of mysteries, as well as forensics experts and law enforcement. With Julie Whitten, she started a group at the West Oakland Senior Center called "Write On," a creative writing workshop originally focused on mysteries, then including all genres of creative writing: poetry, short stories, memoires, etc. Jan would have been delighted to know that these writings would be collected and published in a series of excellent anthologies of seniors' writings.

Jan was a force to be reckoned with—she was brilliant, and fearless. She was a graduate teacher, social worker, and black activist, fighting racism wherever she found it, and promoting equality for the underdog. She was known locally for her museum-quality collection of black memorabilia called Ethnic Notions, and for founding I-Pride, an organization of interracial families/biracial people in support of a positive identity for the many growing multi-ethnic families and communities.

Jan Faulkner

III

About The Editor

Jean Mundy brings to this project more than twenty-seven years as a proofreader. A proud native of Maryland, Jean retired from the City of Oakland twenty years ago. Prior to her employment with the City, Jean worked for two trade advertising agencies, one on the East Coast and the other in California. She has volunteered at the Downtown Oakland Senior Center since 1995 where she works in the Center office four days a week. Jean is a movie lover, and her hobbies include tap dancing, music, reading and staying abreast of current events.

Introduction
by Jennifer King

No matter what's going on in their lives, writers will write. They may not do it every day, but sooner or later, that writing Muse will nag and nag until the writer picks up his or her pen, or turns on the computer, and starts writing. It's a blessing and a curse. The love of weaving words together is hard-wired into the writer. They may see something, or hear a turn of phrase, or perhaps even dream something. Voila, the genesis for a poem or a short story is born. Now, after they have the initial "idea," comes the more difficult part: crafting that idea into a work. Very rarely does the writer get it right the first time. It may take lots of revisions. Often it takes sharing the idea with other writers and getting their input. In any case, it takes work.

The Creative Writing Class at the West Oakland Senior Center knows all about the work involved in creative writing. For the past eight years they have been working at their craft. Weekly workshops involve hours of reading, listening, evaluating, suggesting, coaxing, urging, and, of course, praising—and that's for someone else's work! They are a generous group of writers. They have come to know and understand one another, and they really don't mind taking the time to help one another. Perhaps it's because they understand that when it is their turn, and when their work is being workshopped, their fellow writers will give them the same amount of energy and creativity.

I've often heard (and read) that writing is a solitary art form. One imagines, thinks, dreams and then writes. That may be true, but I have come to believe that really good writing is a product of community, rather than solitude. While one does indeed dream alone, how well that dream is expressed on the page can only be realized if there is a reader. The late African American science fiction novelist Octavia Butler once commented "You don't start out writing good stuff. You start out writing crap and thinking it's good stuff, and then gradually you get better at it." Unless there is a reader, the writer may never know that the first or second draft is "crap." Of course, when we write in a nurturing community of fellow writers —such as the one that has been forged by the writers at the West Oakland Senior Center— what you really have is a gathering of seasoned writing "gardeners." You see, rarely is the issue about writing "crap." Rather, it's like planting a seed and then tending it through thoughtful and helpful criticism. Not only does this type of gardening develop the written piece, it strengthens and bolsters the confidence of the writer.

Week after week, the writers at West Oakland Senior Center bring in their writings and gingerly drop their seeds at the workshop table. Week after week, with respectful support, their fellow writers garden. They help the writer weed out non-productive words, and prune the phrases to tease out a better understanding.

We present you now with the fruits of their labor. In this anthology you see the artful gardeners at their peak. Generations: Life's Journeys is a product of the careful cultivation done in the Creative Writing Workshop at the West Oakland Senior Center. These evocative and sometimes, provocative poems, essays, and short stories allow you to see the writers as they once were, as they now are, and as they hope to be. The characters and situations in this anthology are sometimes fictional. Other times they are autobiographical. Regardless, they are always real and engaging.

Table of Contents

DOUGLAS E. COLEMAN

LUCY ELY

WILLIE FRANCIS

BETTY L. WALKER

JULIANA WHITTEN

Generations
Life's Journeys

Douglas E. Coleman

My birth name is Douglas Eugene Coleman. I am
also known as Katabazi to some. I am a retired
Senior Quality Control Technician for Chevron
Products Co. In this retirement phase of my life I
am a poet and writer. I am also an Elder in my
local community. My poetry and writing is heavily
influenced by the oral traditionists, oral griots
and the Djali men of West Africa. For hundreds
of years, perhaps longer, these human vessels,
these repositories of the history and culture of a
nation held sway until the written script. I also
find encouragement in the poets of The Harlem
Renaissance. Langston Hughes and Claude McKay
are two of my favorites.

I am published in several anthologies but I am
currently in the process of compiling a stand-alone
book of my own.

A COMPLICATED MAN
by Douglas E. Coleman

"You one of those complicated men"
She said with a sly grin, after a count of ten
"I like my men malleable and simple
Easily controlled with a smile and dimple"

Yes I am a complicated man
Doing the best that I can
Your charms are obvious
Well packaged and voluptuous

Yet, questions of life loom large
Beyond the religious charge
I choose my battles
Out of the chatter of nettles

"You use big words and kinda cute
Your words flow like water in a chute
I think you are a real hoot
With some money to boot"

Answers I seek
Above the Earthly Creek
Not for the weak
Nor those prone to splinter and break

"Mmm, you sure talk funny
Warm and cuddly like a bunny
Do you like honey?
Dripping, all golden no boloney"

Yes, I like honey
And I got a little money
I am standing next to you, too
To see what we can do

"I think we can have some fun
After the setting sun
I know a great spot
Called Circle with a Dot"

Yes I know that great place
You lead and I'll match your pace
Then we can swing and sway
Until the break of day

A SUMMER'S ADVENTURE
by Douglas E. Coleman

The summer of 2011 was a time of adventure, fun and accomplishments for me. It began with me entering my fifth year of retirement. At this time the hic-cupping upward direction of the stock market has me optimistic and forward looking. After five years of retirement I was feeling anxious and needing to do something meaningful. That being the case, my thoughts turned to the property in Jamaica. To the 0.8th acre of land on a hill side over looking the low lands of Priory, stretching to the sea. I thought about the unfinished house there, the plush trees, the cool breeze and the quietness so much a part of the aesthetics of the area.

So after working out the details of being away for an extended period of time, with my wife Arlene, I set off for Ocho Rios, Jamaica. I arrived in Ocho Rios in late May on a Tuesday afternoon. I was exhausted from my 15 hours of travel to get there. This was my tenth trip to Ocho Rios over the last 15 years. I quickly unpacked, having mostly brought jeans and white T shirts along with my favorite crushable hat, a pair of sandals and track shoes. I showered and went straight to bed at around 5pm. I slept deeply, some from exhaustion and some from the quiet darkness of the city. There was none of the sounds of police and emergency vehicles racing through the streets.

Wednesday morning I was up and out to take care of banking and to stock the refrigerator with beer and fresh fruits. That afternoon my best friend and business partner, Frankie D. arrived to share the two-bedroom suite at The Fisherman's Point Resort. Although his travel from Oklahoma City had been shorter than mine he was still hot, thirsty and needing the Red Strip beer I pushed into his outstretched hand. It was good to see my old friend. We have known each other for more than 40 years and have been engaged in this building project for more than 10 years now. The building of the house, here in Jamaica, is more than just its completion. It is the interacting with the local community and the working together of two friends who sought to realize a common dream.

The next day we were off to rent a car, then made the trip to the property site. It had been two years since the last clearing, and the tropical growth was tremendous. We contacted Eric, the laborer we used on the property, and asked him to clear the site. Meanwhile Frankie D. and I began to contact building contractors and asked for bids on the building work that we outlined. It had taken four weeks to meet with the various contractors in order to select one to continue the building on the house. By that time Frankie D. had exhausted his vacation time and had to return to the States. I estimated that I could remain another six weeks during which I would get as much done on the house that time and funds would allow. I saw Frankie D. off as he boarded the large air-conditioned bus back to the airport. This time it was me seeing him off, whereby in the past he has seen me off. Over the following weeks I missed and longed for my friend as his knowledge and home building experience was better than mine. Additionally we enjoy being together and our partnership in the house was a reflection of the bond.However, before he left, he and I were out one afternoon trying to find some shrimp-fried rice to eat. We were disappointed that two of our favorite restaurants that served great shrimp-fried rice had closed. So, while in search of the dish, by chance we stopped at a seafood restaurant at a small community outside of Ocho Rios called Discovery Bay. The restaurant manager graciously agreed to prepare dishes for the two of us, as it was not on the menu. While there we entered into casual conversations with the restaurant manager, a delightful Jamaican lady of some 60 years, who revealed her desire to produce a poetry program at the restaurant. Soon a friend of hers stopped by for food but joined the conversation. During the conversation I mentioned that I was a published poet and writer. I had a copy of one of my books with me. In this case it was *Mosaics*. The friend, a writer, read my poem aloud, *The Yearning Heart*. It was interesting to listen to her read my words and to hear her voice catch the rhythm

7

of the poem, revealing creeping interest as the next line speaks. Both the manger and friend liked the poem. They implored me to join with them and some friends to help them get the poetry program off. I reluctantly agreed as I have a building project to oversee. However, I supported their goal to present something different in the area for older mature adults. New meeting dates were set for further developing.

Meanwhile back at the building site I have to manage building materials and finances as well as my lodging and substance. My job as owner was to have materials and tools available for the workers. I wanted the work to continue at an uninterrupted pace. I used all local workers and services on the building site. After two weeks I moved out of the suite at The Point and into a residential apartment. It was in a local neighborhood of Ocho Rios. The daily rate was about 40% less than that at the resort. I ate in the local restaurants and shopped for food at local supermarkets. I greeted and had conversations with locals at the apartment, on the streets at markets, and clubs. Most were very nice and in some cases showed deference, which I attribute in part to my age, gray hair and repeated trips to the city. Americans who visit Jamaica frequently are sometimes referred to as Jamerican, a term of some endearment.

After three weeks on the island I let the rental car go and used route cabs to go about like the locals who did not own cars. I became a recognizable figure as the American with hat, bag, blue jeans and white T shirt. My gray mustache earned me the status of "Dada," a title of respect for senior males. As I didn't have a car, I walked a lot under the Jamaican sun and that helped me to maintain physical conditioning without having to workout at a gym.

Early one Sunday morning, after a late Saturday night of activities, I received a call from Lea, one of the poetry coordinators: she charged me to join her at Ocho Rios's premier radio station, Ire FM 107.7, to promote and talk about the upcoming poetry program. I did not know where the radio station was and tried to beg off, but Lea would not have it. After receiving directions to the radio station I made my way there in the rental car that I had for the day. Lea joined me there and after a brief period we went into the broadcast studio. I was introduced as an American poet appearing on the program and asked to share a poem. This time I read *The Yearning Heart*. I read it with passion. I sought to bring to the radio audience the feelings and emotions that had produced the poem. It was very well received. I was pleased.

Back at the work site it was at the chief point of the construction, the pouring of the roof slab. In Jamaica houses are built from steel and concrete cinder blocks. The slab, the covering for the lower level ceiling, is six inches thick with half-inch steel bars throughout. The pouring of the cement over the steel bars is done in a continuous process, requiring the presence of 25 workers. Workers push wheelbarrows after wheelbarrows of wet cement to the cement finisher, who works the wet cement with some urgency. This process is repeated until the slab pouring is complete. The slab requires the underneath support of dozens of support-studs to support the six inch, heavy-wet slab above. With the slab poured most work is halted for three days while the slab dries and hardens. I now had more time to work on the poetry program. I lent my insights to the program, talked it up to locals and passed out flyers. Finally the day of the program was here. I was scheduled to present in the middle of the program. Each presenter was allotted about twenty minute. I recited three poems: *Some Say*, *A Simple Poet* and *The Yearning Heart*. I read one of my short stories, *Troubling Waters*, from *Mosaics*. My presentation was very well received and I was pleased by the outpouring of applause and appreciation. I was welcomed and well received.

The next day I attended a gathering, at the home of Lea, one of the organizing ladies. Other members of the organizing group were there as well. Lea has a large beautiful home that sits on well-kept grounds filled with trees and flowers. We critiqued the program and felt the program was indeed a success. I was thanked for work and participation. Additionally, I was told that I was now a part of the Discovery Bay community. I was no longer a foreigner.

I left Jamaica after 10 weeks, feeling that I had entered into a new relationship with the island that I love. The work on the house is still unfinished but I live with the knowledge that the next time it will be easier. The new friends that I made, their acceptance of me as one of their own and a new motivation to see the house completed.

IN MEMORY OF MR. BOONE
by Douglas E. Coleman

The voice of a poet goes silent
Memories, deeds and words continue on out loud
Life bobbing on *The Tide of Time*
Sometimes smooth sailing
Other times tossed and driven
I burn incense
That your life be founded pleasing
I pour water to the ground
That your soul be welcomed
I strike once on *The Bar of Truth*
Reaffirming that Truth sustains all

STEP, STEP, STEPPING STONES
by Douglas E. Coleman

(Author's comments)
This essay appeared in **Stepping Stones: An Anthology of Creative Writings by Seniors, vol. 3** *in 2009. I have added additional comments in sections as updates and additional commentary.*

Steeping Stones we tread. Steeping Stones we become. If I had the listening ear of the world's youth, I would tell them that I am sorry. I am sorry that those of us alive today, as well as those that came before us, were unable to deliver to them a world free of hate, violence and war. But like them we inherited the world as it is **with all its chaos, violence and destruction. We also inherited the beauty of nature and its teachings.** Each generation borrows from the previous generation and attempts to build on what is received. "That's the way things are..." so often heard among people today but somehow the statement fails to give proper weight to earlier contributions and the timing of their arrival. Such as: **the spoken word and its understood and accepted meaning, the use of words to preserve information**, establishing an alphabet, a written language, mathematics, measuring systems etc... Yes, these systems have been improved upon over time by following generations but these refiners did not originate the fundamental ideas that ignited the processes. **Early systems of language, mathematics and measuring systems grew out of the need to organize increased numbers of people living in a common union**.

Within the notion of Stepping Stones and accumulated historical data we can look back at segments of our human journey, some 250,000-150,000 years ago for modern man. With the comforts of modern societies today, do we dare look back to the periods of Savagery and Barbarism? It is almost universally accepted, that our human ancestors lived through those earlier and grave periods to give rise to our current societies. **Humans do not live very long as a specie so the ability to pass information along to succeeding generations is a great victory. We should acknowledge the human journey as a common experience unique to our specie.**

The Period of Savagery:

The definitions of Savagery and Barbarism are not universally accepted by all who have studied the matter. However, Dr. John G. Jackson in his *Man, God and Civilization*, sites the definitions of the anthropologist, Lewis Henry Morgan and Dr. Jackson's selection is fine with me. For my purposes here I will paraphrase Dr. Morgan's definitions. Dr. Morgan defines Savagery in three terms: Lower Savagery, Middle Savagery and Upper Savagery. Lower Savagery reflects the early beginnings of humans, having separated themselves from other primates. They wandered in small groups subsisting on a diet of fish, nuts and berries. Humans later acquired speech and an expanded sense of self awareness over a period of thousands of years. In the latter years of Lower Savagery and moving into early Middle Savagery humans are found using and making fire. **The use of fire was a great victory for humans at this time. Fire allowed them to cook raw food and to metabolize it into greater muscle growth and clearer thinking.** Still later the bow and arrow was acquired during Upper Savagery and humans began to spread out over the lands. **The bow and arrow allowed humans to hunt and kill large animals from a distance. The addition of meat protein to the diet allowed humans to grow stronger with additional energy. These early victories increased their confidence and feed their innovations with better weaponry.**

The Period of Barbarism:

In Lower Barbarism we find humans making pottery, domesticating animals and building stone houses. Middle Barbarism introduced the smelting of iron ore while the process was refined in Upper Barbarism into making iron implements. **This led to** better farming implements which produced greater food production. Again better weaponry was realized as well. An alphabet was introduced during this period and writing followed.

(The notion of Civilization is being withheld at this time).

In the earlier edition of this essay I wrote the above statement in regard to Civilization. I now site the definition of Dr. Morgan which he calls, *Status of Civilization*: "this period began with the use of a phonetic alphabet and the art of producing literary records and continues to this time." I choose to list the definition at this time because it is open and general. It includes none of the typical romantic ideas about civilized and civilization so easily found today in pop culture. The standards of Civilization should be held high and should preclude the practitioners of large-scale wars and hoarders of extreme wealth.

Some of the dates and definitions cited above may be disputed, but my purpose in citing the periods of Savagery and Barbarism is to **acknowledge** the trek of human history and to illustrate the concept of stepping stones. Modernity did not emerge spontaneously, intact as we know it today. First, within the notion of Stepping Stones is to show the long human experience that it has taken to get to our current societies. Secondly, I want to show the common humanity **that binds us all together on this small planet**.

I began the discussion with the human experience at the stage of human Savagery with the idea of avoiding any conflicts between the theories of Evolution and Creationism. All human generations acquire from the past and deliver to the present/future. Each generation going forward expands the human conscientiousness to embrace new ideas as possibilities rooted in the achievements of past generations as well as the new discoveries of the day.

Those of us alive today and following generations are fortunate in that we are able to look back at the history of our ancient ancestors with increasing depth and clarity. New anthropological discoveries are still being unearthed in Africa and other parts of the world. The unraveling of archaic languages and the human genome system continues. **The Human Genome Project was completed in April 2003**. Humans are looking deeper and venturing further into the outer cosmos than ever before. **The probe, Curiosity, landed on Mars in 2012 and is now returning data**.

Here, on Earth, human populations continue to increase. Global economies are increasingly more intertwined, bringing different cultures into greater contact. **Cultural differences often pose challenges to established hegemonies and the common humanity disappears**. Competition among industrialized nations for finite resources, to drive modern industrialization expansionism, will keep global tensions edgy in the near future. **Growing environmental concerns will add new tensions to the volatile mix**. Can humans rise above the cycles of famine and war? Enlighten thinkers will agree that it is our common humanity, in all of its diversity, that binds us together. The unknown vastness **and mystery** of outer space illuminates our **tiny size**, isolation and perhaps uniqueness. Even if other life forms are encountered they probably will not look like us or share our world view. Enlighten Thinkers must openly promote dialogue that places the common humanity of all humans at the center of the national and international dialogue.

It is human beings that have emerged out of a process of "stepping stones" to lead the inhabitants of Earth. This should not be taken lightly as I have attempted to show the long hard slog of the human experience through Savagery, Barbarism **and into Civilization**. These periods covered more than 250,000 years, a brief period of time relative to the age of Earth. Still, with the relative short life span of humans, the climb has been driven and steady. The concept of "stepping stones," being played out again and again. **Generation after generation**.

Humans appear to be the only life forms on Earth capable of unraveling the mysteries of life. All the while the day to day realities of living are married to the time of each generation.

There may come a time when the nations of the worlds will have to work together to save the world. As more is learned about our planet and universe, perhaps more will be revealed as to our past and future.

When we can look beyond the race, color and religious affiliation of humans and see the common humanity as the highest good, we will position ourselves to better unravel the mysteries of life, which is: Who are we? Why are we here? Where are we going?

A TASTE OF THE BITTER SWEET
by Douglas E. Coleman

In 1968, while serving the final year of a four-year enlistment in the U.S. Air Force, I was assigned to the Mill Valley Air Force Station. The station was on a site on the upper level of Mt. Tamalpais in Mill Valley, California. An Air Force station differs from a military base in the number of personnel assigned to it. Air Force stations typically have fewer than 3,000 service personnel and tend to be isolated from civilian populations. The Mill Valley Air Force Station was a radar site. It had only about 280 airmen stationed there. 1968 would begin my final year in the Air Force although I was not certain of that at the time. I had recently arrived at the Mill Valley Air Force Station having just completed a rough one-year-isolated-remote tour in Alaska. The Alaska assignment had been at an Air Force station well situated in the Aleutian Islands Chain on Niska Island, second from the last island in the chain.

California in 1968 was a striking and welcoming change from the dull, gray dreariness on Niska Island. Right away I loved the Bay Area weather, the roar and sway of the Pacific Ocean, different ethnic groups, the sounds and cadence of their speech and the proximity of many different cities. There were the smells and aromas of different foods that were so inviting. The blast of different musical sounds seemly spawned new dance styles every few months. I was not quite 21 on my arrival to California, driving my sleek black 1966 Chevy Impala. The energy of the Bay Area was typified by that of the Haight/Asbury people gatherings, Sausalito's Bridge Way Park, Berkeley's People Park, and Oakland's Eastmont Mall. The energy that spoke to me was that most people were into getting along and that was fine with me. It was a relief to be free from the physical and mental demands of the Alaska tour. Near the end of my tour in Alaska, I had requested a California assignment as my first choice. The Air force makes no promises on assignments, as the needs of the Air Force came first. However, they found the Mill Valley Air Force Station within 25 miles of my first choice. I was grateful for the accommodation.

With my arrival I immediately threw myself into my work at the radar site as an Airman Third Class, 5 Level Refrigeration and Air-Conditioning Specialist. It too was a small section. There was a civilian supervisor, a second-class airman and me, a third-class airman. I was working with the supervisor and through correspondence courses, for my 7 level technician grade which was advanced work given my three years of active duty. The supervisor readily turned over to me the training of the Airman Second Class. The young airman had failed on his two previous attempts to pass the test for his 5 level classifications. The refrigeration and air conditioning section was keen on training and classification levels are tied to rank promotion. The achievement of higher skill levels by trainees may be viewed as positive or negative reflection on the trainer and trainee. I worked closely with the young airman for several weeks before his next test date. I was particularly pleased when the airman passed the test on his next effort under my tutelage.

One day after work, as I moved about the station, I encountered several airmen who approached me and asked, if I had checked the promotion listings. I had not, so my answer was no. They said "Man, you made staff!" meaning I was promoted to the rank of staff sergeant. I was genuinely shocked and surprised once I checked the promotion listings and saw for myself. There was my name under the "Promoted to Staff Sergeant" heading. My shock and surprise was fueled by the fact that few enlistees were promoted to the rank of staff sergeant under four years and with minimum time in grade. My older brother was in the Air Force as well. He had entered two years ahead of me and had not made "staff" yet. It was my brother who had given me the confidence that I could handle the military life offered by the Air Force. Our joining the Air Force was either that or be drafted into the Army with a fox-hole offering in Vietnam. My brother during a career went on to achieve the rank of Chief Master Sergeant, the highest enlistee rank in the Air Force. Later in the day, several airmen came by my room to congratulate me. Some of them had 9 to 12 years in military service and still had not made "staff." Some were bitter and made a point of castigating me for my newly acquired rank. Some were incensed given my youth and brief military service, that I would be promoted to staff. Several of the men were on their third four-year enlistment.

I understood the disappointment of those severing many years in the Air Force and seemly not to get recognition. I felt both elated and regretful with my new rank. Until the promotion listings had come out I had held no inkling that I would achieve the rank of staff sergeant in three years. I was thinking more along the average of six to seven years, if I stayed in. I could not change the circumstances of my brother and the other airmen who had yet to be promoted to the rank of staff sergeant. The rank of staff sergeant in the Air Force was in many ways a turning point for those on the military career track. The rank of staff was typically offered during the second four-year enlistment, often as an incentive to sign on for another four years. The rank officially placed one among the non-commissioned officers category. There was a decent pay increase, added privileges, greater acceptance among peer NCOs, while offering first-time enlistees hope for their rank possibilities.

Because of Air force security protocols at the time and my expectation to leave the military at the end of my enlistment, I rarely shared with my friends, family and colleagues my service record while serving on dreary Niska Island. I never told them how at the age of 19, and three months after my arrival on Niska Island, I was summoned to my department commander's office. On my arrival the commander was quick to the point. He told me that my section supervisor (a civilian) had a family emergency and was returning to the lower "forty-eight" tomorrow morning, if the weather permitted. He went on to say that between me and Braxton, the other airmen third class assigned to the section, I held one month time in-grade in rank over him. That made me the senior airmen third class and I was in charge of the refrigeration and air-conditioning section. I would have the authority of a Non-Commissioned Officer in Charge (NCOIC), typically a Tech-sergeant, three stripes down and two stripes up along with two pay grades above my own. The Refrigeration/Air-Conditioning Section on Niska included the Krypto Room, General Electric Section, the cold storage plant and all freezers and ice cream makers in the Housing Compound Cafeteria. The commander said that he realized that I was young and new to the island. He said that he regretted the short notice. That he was actively pursuing the supervisor's replacement with a higher ranking experienced sergeant. He was requesting that a replacement be sent right away but that it might take three or four months to secure the serviceman. He went on to say that in the interim I was in charge; there were no other personnel from other sections that had the training to assist us. That we were on our own and to do the best that we could. Reflecting on the exchange I can't imagine what the commander (rank of major) thought. Standing before him was a 19-year-old kid with a 5 level skill rating, recently promoted to airman third class and just two years of Air Force service. The refrigeration and air condition section played a pivotal support role to the mission. He could not have been filled with optimism. I left the meeting with the commander a bit shaken and feeling uncertain. It's funny I remember feeling like I felt when I was 13 and stepping to the podium during the State Regional Public-Speaking Competition. Though nervous at first, I found my calm and delivered the first-place winning presentation. Now, I would have to trust that Braxton and I together could solve the various and unknown problems that we may face.

I never mentioned to others, in the subsequent months the many dark and early morning hours when Braxton and I went out into the blinding snow and freezing cold to switch over the electrical power at the cold storage plant from line power to auxiliary power. This action was necessary and had to be implemented in stages every time a bad storm was forecast to be coming our way, which was often. The bad storms would often take down commercial power lines. If this occurred before we switched to auxiliary power the three-phase motors on the many freezers refrigeration units would single-phase and burn out. The cold storage plant held six months of emergency food reserves for the 2500 Air Force station personnel. Given the unpredictable weather of the region it could be months sometimes before a supply plane could safely land on the island. The island had the Pacific Ocean on its south side and the Bering Sea on the north side. The dissimilar water temperatures between the two bodies of waters coming together created continuous fog over the island that blocked the sunshine year round, producing a gray dreariness that was depressingly always there.

I never mentioned the section's successful passing of inspection from the Office of the Inspector General. I did not speak of the security scrimmages with M-16 on the frozen tundra every time a Soviet ship appeared on the horizon or the eyes-on-you whenever we went to the Kryto Room to service the air-conditioning unit. The Krypto Room was our number one priority and the equipment had to be repaired quickly and on the spot. The Krypto Room housed some of the earliest versions of the computer. Then, they were large bulky units, always covered during our visits. The room was kept cool. These early generations of the computer gave off a lot of heat and operated best in an environment where the temperature was maintained about 65 degrees. Once in the Krypto Room one could not leave until the equipment was repaired. There was no returning to the vehicle for parts or equipment. It was necessary to try to anticipate what the problem might be from the service request. Then carry the necessary parts and tools in to the room all at once. Sometimes this required assistance from the personnel of the Krypto Room.

Even today, I rarely speak of the eleven months, two weeks and three days of the dreary day-to-day experiences on the island. There was the remote-isolation of the experience. All personnel services and lodging was in a single three-level compound in the shape of a capital (I). There were no trees or flowers on Niska Island, only tundra plants. The only animals were sea gulls. There was the noticeable lack of sunshine on the skin of black, white and all colors in between. There were no women on the island, no rest and recuperation (R&R) granted owing to the high rate of airmen failing to return to the island. I was aware of at least three airmen who cracked under the mental strain of the isolation during my tour. In spite of the difficulties endured, Airman Third Class Braxton and I, held our own in support of the mission at the height of the Cold War with the Soviet Union.

No, I never mentioned any of this to my colleagues at the Mill Valley Air Force Station in an effort to justify my new rank. I had nine months left in the Air Force and I was getting out. However, I would take with me the memories of hard-smart work, the ability to perform under pressure, and the satisfaction of knowing that while I was simply going about my tasks, doing the best that I could, my efforts had not gone unnoticed and my commanders from Niska and Mill Valley A.F.S. had sought to reward that work by recommending me for the rank of Staff Sergeant.

After nine months I was honorably discharged from the U.S. Air Force at the age of 21. I left feeling that I had been tested and now I was ready to take on the next phase of my life as a civilian again.

TWEAKING
by Douglas E. Coleman

People in metropolitan areas all over the world were becoming increasingly dull, rude, incommunicable, impulsive, introverted and robotic. Even with casual observations, thousands of people at any given moment could be found with a wireless phone to their ear. It seems that humanity itself was under attack and facing a grave threat. The background music in the quiet restaurant was a familiar commercial track, a mixture of contemporary pop and old-school Rhythm & Blues. There were only a few customers in the dining area and like the people on the mall thoroughfare, most were engaged with some kind of electronic device. Some wore earplugs while others held the phone to their ear. It was Saturday, about noon. The sun was bright and the sky was clear as Frank David entered the mall. He soon found his favorite restaurant and table. Frank sat at the window table with an open notebook, looking as casual as he could. He was dressed in tan slacks, a blue crew-neck sweater and light brown jacket. He wore his favorite brown Kangol cap and had his well-worn bag in the adjoining chair. His cell phone, with the battery removed, was tucked away in an inside pocket. The window opened to the mall thoroughfare. Frank was in a moderate-size California city but it would have been the same any place else. He was sipping a cup of green mint tea and making entries in the notebook. His entries were coded, using the system that he learned with the Watchers. He was watching the mall people stroll by, most with a wireless phone to their left ear. This restaurant was one of Frank's favorite locations for watching and recording the number of people that passed his view and "tweaked." He recorded the exact time from his synchronized watch as close as he could. He had other viewing locations but this was one of his favorites. The number of people that passed the window within an hour and "tweaked" gave the statisticians at the Den a representative number of people infected with the an electronic bug and the rate of increase of the infection. Others at the Den, computer and technical people,

23

are working feverish to find a fix for the electronic bug. It is a highly calibrated frequency pulse. The frequency pulse coming through the human ear canal affected that section of the brain in a way that made the subconscious mind open to suggestions. A nano-second after the frequency pulse an audio message is sent "work, be productive." Where and what was its source? They all were working to solve the mystery.

Frank David (Frankie D.) to his few remaining friends and survivors that are not infected by the electronic bug, felt that this new disease was quickly infecting the world's populations. The infection produces subtle changes in human behavior that is called "tweaking" by the Watchers. Tweaking is the sudden onset of a pause or hesitation in whatever the situation while talking on a wireless phone. During the pause the face goes blank, taking on an ashen appearance with a slight jerking of the head, always to the left. It is believed by the Watchers to be the point of delivery of the electronic bug.

The Watchers are a small group of men and women of various ages and races bound together by being uninfected, recognizing that others are infected, and that the infection was being orchestrated by others. Frank was a part of the Watchers. He had been recruited two years ago after months of monitoring by the Watchers. Frank was an African American, fifty two years old, 5'9" and 180 lbs. He was a retired major of the U.S. Air Force and has never been married. As a career officer, marriage did not fit him. He knew other career officers who had families but he felt a different calling. Frank was intelligent, disciplined and cared about people, especially the working-class. His life today was not connected to his active-duty years, except for his firm self-discipline and keen mind. The firm discipline was one of the reasons that his relations with women had never lasted more than a few months. Most of the women he had dated found him too demanding. Frank was an insatiable reader and fitness enthusiast as well. During the seven years that he has been retired he has served as a local community activist. He focused on one community: teaching African history, giving political analysis and organizing the community to vote. It was this work that had brought him to the attention of the Watchers. He was observant, and a critical thinker. Frank had lived and traveled long enough to recognize that things where changing in the social fabric of American life. As America goes, so does much of the rest of the industrialized world. Human interactions were fading while electronic engagement was increasing. He did not believe that this was a good change. As a teacher of history he was aware of the brutality and violence that had gone into the development of human societies. He has travelled extensively throughout the world: Africa, South America, Europe and the Caribbean. Over the last ten years he began to notice that people, mostly in metropolitan areas but in others as well, were engaging in strange and exaggerated behavior at odd times.The tweaking infection caused impulsive and exaggerate behavior in public or social gatherings. It is particularly telling on some of the youth. The exaggeration was most noticeable in American urban cities. Today's youth, having been acculturated in the electronic age, used electronics with abandonment but they lacked the benefits of maturity. Many of these youth, mostly African-American, have taken to wearing oversized pants, refused to wear a belt or set their pants to the waistline where most pants are designed to be worn. They often engaged in the practice of holding their pants up with one hand or simply allowing them to sag to mid-buttock. Without hip support the wearers are forced to spread their legs to keep the pants from crumpling at their feet. Some have taken to wearing the pants sagging with a belt at mid-thigh. This, of course, reduces mobility and changes the natural gait of walking to a waddle. Human beings walk upright and stride in balance. It is a positive attribute. Despite all encouragement to pull their pants up, these "saggers" continue this strange practice.

Serial killers and murder-suicide episodes have spiked among many white adults and youth. It seems their intolerance for life's disappointments made it preferable to kill and die rather than to face the events and circumstances of daily life. Life is hard for all and it is becoming harder for the less fortunate and less prepared. Indeed there was a spike in murder-suicides among all groups: men, women, black, white and others. These killers, having grown weary and fed-up with disappointments took up powerful arms to settle old scores, to end the pain that made life going forward impossible. From school playgrounds to corporate board rooms citizens sought justice through the gun. Yet through all the chaos the workers remained productive on their jobs. The stock exchanges reached all-time highs. New millionaires and billionaires were added to the list of the wealthy every year. But at the other end of the economic scale, millions of middle-class Americans were forced into a lower standard of living. Those Americans already caught in the grip of a low standard of living were forced into deeper poverty and homelessness. There was a great mental fog before the people. This mental fog diminished vision and shrouded truth. People increasingly put their energies and interactions into machines and gadgets, that is, when they were not on the job.

Tweaking was often manifested in road rage with gun battles taking place on freeways. The incidents of murder-suicides were cutting down innocent victims with impunity. Still, workers were productive and the stock exchanges were at an all-time high. Some of the productivity was owing to the diminished power of workers' unions and the increasing power of corporations. Cities across the nation were experiencing increased crime and a breakdown in the social order. Most corporations were huge and had grown in their global influence. They pursued economic gain over nationalism and they showed little commitment to American workers. Elected national representatives no longer adhered to the wishes of the people who elected them but operated to sustain and empower the corporations. It was the curious irony of the unappreciated productive worker and the continuous growth of corporations and the corporate elites that were a concern to the Watchers. It is this observation, in part, that feed the notion that tweaking was being orchestrated by corporate elites. That and Bill Killion. Killion had been a member of the manipulating corporate elites. The story told to the members of the Watchers was that Killion, after a search of conscience and some newfound spiritual awareness, left the elites and exposed their plot. The plot was to control world production through the workers using a calibrated electronic pulse and audio message delivered by wireless phone communications. The elites sought a productive worker who would consistently show up for work, not complain about the working conditions and accept the labor packages offered. It had taken them several years with the work of some of the best program engineers in the world to design the electronic pulse. The electronic bug was a calibrated frequency pulse with an audio message that was designed to impact a part of the brain that would accept new programming. The new programming to the recipient was to "work, be productive." It was entirely possible that the elites themselves had become infected by the bug as they displayed ruthless tactics in trampling on the rights of individuals and nations. They took private lands and natural resources from any place on the planet that offered the prospects of turning a profit. The elites unleashed a torrid public response to Killion's revelation of their plot. They attacked and discredited him as a lunatic. He was driven underground. People being fed a steady stream of the electronic bug were unable to think critically, thus the mental fog. Over time as Killion revealed the plot of the elites to selected individuals he found a reaffirming and engaged audience. There were men and women who had long suspected as much from their own observations and seer intuition. They were free thinkers and unimpressed with the latest electronic devices.

Frank folded his notebook and left the restaurant. He had seen enough for today. He got into his old Chevy Impala parked in the last stall of the parking lot. It was an open lot that afforded Frank a view to see if he was being observed or followed. He drove out of the parking lot and made several turns and reversals to thaw any attempts to follow him. It was protocol for all members of the Watchers. Several minutes later he arrived at the Den. The Den was an old nondescript warehouse to the outside viewer, but the building was completely autonomous. It had its own electric power and water supply. The building held many functions for the Watchers. There were several loft spaces where a few members lived full time. They maintained the building and provided security. There was also some sophisticated electronic gadgetry there to aid in pinpointing the main control centers of the elites. The Den was where the briefings and meetings were held for the Watchers. Meetings were held only when deemed necessary, otherwise they gathered or communicated minimally.

All Watchers carried cell phones, rarely on their person but usually in a bag with the battery removed. When making a call the battery was installed and the conversation was held to 35 seconds or less.

A story frequently told to newly recruited Watchers was the story of Tim Ford. Tim was a recent recruit to the Watchers, having been with the group less than two years. One evening, a few minutes before 6 pm, Tim received information through his network of friends and associates that his mother was gravely ill. As a Watcher, Tim had severed all ties with family and friends who were not in the Watchers. Tim did not want to involve others in his activities. He loved his mother and longed to hear her voice once more. He reasoned that a quick call to her would enliven her spirits as well as his own. Tim knew that the "bug" was dispersed randomly throughout the 24-hour day. The desire to hear her voice and to reassure her of his safety was paramount. Quickly he removed the cell phone and battery from his back pack. He looked at passersby suspiciously; quickly he inserted the battery and dialed his mother's number. That was the worst time for Tim to use the phone because it was it that moment that the bug was dispersed and Tim Ford was infected. Just as his mother answered and said hello, the electronic pulse came through, followed by the statement "work, be productive." He was later observed by a fellow Watcher walking into active traffic, talking on a wireless phone. Tim never saw the SUV, nor did the driver of the SUV see Tim as they both were talking on wireless phones. The SUV struck Tim at full speed, killing him instantly and tossing his wireless phone high into the air. The driver of the SUV lost control of his phone; it was flung from his hand. Both phones were in flight, spinning and rotating as if unaffected by gravity. But the force of gravity did prevail and brought the phones to the hard asphalt surface with sharp cracking sounds. Both phones came apart, their scattered parts framing the bloody mangled body of Tim Ford.

New recruits usually got the message. Some said that the story was a fake, but whether true or false the story had a telling effect on the recruits and that was the purpose.

Observations Reports are dropped off weekly at a central location at the Den. Watchers strive to blend in, to appear as part of the normal. Watchers hoped to break the electronic tether that the elites have on the world populations. Except for some of the European countries, the rest of the world populations lived at bare minimum, acquiring just enough, in the form of food and lodging, to keep working every day. The Watchers also wanted to calm the social order that was just short of complete chaos. Theirs was the voice of reason in moments of conflict. It was believed that the elites knew of the side effects of the electronic bug. That it produced the impulsive or exaggerated behavior at various times, except while on the job. This made the living conditions in most communities hellish. Verbal insults between groups and individuals were hurled seemingly at every opportunity. There was the strange debate between some misguided blacks and white supremacists on the use of the N-word. Some blacks argued that they can use the N-word but whites cannot. Yet they agreed that it sounded similar when spoken but they spell the word differently. They spell the word with an 'ah' on the end instead of "ger" and at that point the word takes on a meaning of endearment. Like homie, buddies, best friends between and among blacks and selected non-blacks that use the N-word in the same way. Somehow homie, buddy and best friend are just not sufficient to convey the great swell of fondness and admiration that the N-word does. It continues to be a mystery why some blacks cling to the use of the N-word while most blacks feel the word should be allowed to die. White bigots countered that it was their ancestors who created the word in the first place. They proudly proclaimed that they, like their ancestors, poured all the spite, disdain and hate that they could muster into that word and "by God" they were not about to leave it solely in the mouths of a bunch of N-word with "ah" or otherwise. So the curious debate went back and forth, both sides clinging to and keeping the N-word alive.

Some street walkers were in an uproar with the show performances of some the top female pop performers. They argued that these vixens were stealing their styles and moves, and they wanted it to stop. The adopting of styles popularized by prostitutes were forcing prostitutes to go to greater extremes in order to draw attention to themselves. Many of these ladies of the night appeared on dark urban streets with bra and thong alone. They insisted that the dress of some of the pop stars was influencing dress among high schoolers, college students and "hot moms." Some young women dressed so provocative that indeed some were indistinguishable from street walkers. Violent confrontations erupted regularly between johns seeking service and skimpily-clad young women allegedly going about their business. The young women proclaimed their rights to dress as they pleased and to be free of harassment. The johns claimed that it was too hard to determine who was who and there needed to be clearer guidelines. So, another unresolved conflict that fed into the violent dysfunction of most cities.

The elites knew of the side effects of the electronic bug but viewed it as tolerable, as part of the cost of doing business. Elites were able to isolate themselves from the general public with high walls, chauffeured limousines and personal security. They only socialized and interacted with other elites. They all shared the common vision of power, control and materialism. They believed that they and their descendants would exhaust the resources of Earth and then seek an off-Earth home. They were well into the research of space colonies and living in outerspace. The elites were confident that they could continue their lives of opulence in outerspace, while controlling things on Earth and seeking a new home planet. The elites believed they were in charge of Earth, its resources, most of the world's populations and they had every intention of maintaining that relationship. They were aware of the Watchers and similar groups but did not consider them a major threat. They frequently cursed Killion for his betrayal. He had once been part of them and shared in the opportunities that they reserved for themselves. He would be assassinated if his whereabouts was determined. But the slippery bastard and his ragtail group was difficult to find.

The Watchers knew of their dastardly plan and were acting to stop it. The researchers at the Den thought that they were close to designing a counter pulse that would stop the delivery of the audio message. Meanwhile, the Watchers continued to monitor the public and to search for candidates to join them in the resistance.

The Den was all a buzz with laughter and toasting glasses when Frank arrived. He had received notice to return to the Den for a special announcement. Everyone seemed to be looking and pointing at Frank when Stan Simmons, the Den director, came running up to Frank and gave him a big hug. Stan called for quietness. When the room grew quiet, Stan said that they had a major breakthrough on the bug infestation. He said that Frank's very consistent and detailed entries had revealed a clear pattern among the Tweakers he recorded in a particular region. The computer engineers were able to design a counter virus that disrupted the frequency of the electronic pulse and sent it on a reverse trace to the center of the origin of the pulse. The counter virus alters the frequency of the electronic pulse and the suggested message can't get through. Gradually the suggested message loses its grip on the minds of the infected. Stan says that early results indicated the counter virus has a long reach and that results were being reported in regions thought to be unrelated to the primary region. Due to Frank's diligence the patterns had revealed themselves and now the Watchers and the uninfected could take the offense by reclaiming their lives and minds. Frank was completely surprised by the gathering and congratulations from his colleagues. He thanked them and joined in the celebration, pleased that his efforts had borne results. Frank threw himself into the celebration and was surprised by his own elation.

For many years the Watchers had worked to defeat the bug that drained away peoples' humanity. Now, weeks in the aftermath of the destruction of the bugs' centers around the world, people again could be seen talking face to face without a cell phone in sight. This renewed behavior could be seen in cars, on subways, buses, coffee shops, in parks, etc. Laughter, long absent from human interactions, now filled the public places. Labor unions and nonunion workers were challenging the corporate elites on old-bug-inspired labor contracts. Angry workers wanted all labor contracts revised and updated. Since the outerspace colonies were not yet a reality many of the elites were on the move in deeper seclusion and security. The plot was foiled and coming apart. Bill Killion had come out of hiding as many elites went into hiding. Killion was receiving new attention from a sober and embarrassed media. He was telling it all. How a decade ago several powerful elites had gathered in a secluded wilderness retreat and planned the electronic pulse attack. Each year they would return to the wilderness retreat with additional members and the current progress on the electronic pulse. Many corrupt politicians were arguing that they had been under the influence of the bug and were not fully responsible for their bad actions. A nice try, but clearer thinking people did not believe it and the offending politicians were immediately kicked out of office. The politicians who remained knew that they were under high scrutiny and they moved surprisingly quickly with legislation to break up and sell off large corporate holdings. Some of the corporations were purchased by the workers and profit sharing programs were set up. There was a noticeable decrease in all categories of crime. Yes, it seemed that trends towards normalcy were well under way.

The Watchers were slowly disbanding. Members were renewing and returning to families not seen in years. Frank had reached out to his brothers and sisters. He had not seen them in three years and was pleased that he was welcomed back into the fold. In fact he was something of a hero to his family and the nation.

Still, months into the recovery from the bug, some things were relatively unchanged. Many youth still wore sagging pants and the conflict as to who could use the N-word continued. But now there is hope where a few months ago there had been very little.

Lucy Ely

I was born to the proud parents of Mary and Daniel Jenkins in Mobile, Alabama. I am the sixth of 16 children. I am the mother of three children, two sons and one daughter. I migrated to California in 1969 and recieved a degree from Cal State University in liberal arts and received a masters degree from Nova University. I taught school for 36 years before retiring in 2003. I am currently a student of creative writing at the West Oaklnd Senior Center. I am also a Sunday School teacher for the women at my church.

A BAD TRIP GOING NOWHERE
by Lucy Ely

I was a high school senior attending Mobile County Training School in Mobile, Alabama in the year of 1956. When I became a senior, I thought I was the "top of the line," and I couldn't wait to graduate. I was sure nothing was going to stop me. I was so foolish I thought I could walk on top of the moon.

My mother had warned me about not having sex, smoking cigarettes, drinking alcohol, or shooting dice like the boys used to do. She had also told us not to smoke marijuana, but I thought because I was a senior I could try it and get by with it.

My girlfriend approached me one morning and said, "Lucy, I got some good stuff. Child, you need to try it!" I said, "If it's that good I'll try it and see what it tastes like."

Our school had just gotten new indoor bathrooms with new toilets and face bowls. I told my girlfriend and two other friends that we would meet in the bathroom at lunch time and try the good stuff. I watched my girlfriends puff the marijuana and I said I wanted to be last. I was thinking I would smoke up all the rest of it by myself. They took their puffs and nothing happened to them. They were having a good time, and I thought I could have a good time too.

My girlfriend handed me the weed. I took one puff. It seemed like something went up my nose and cut my breathing off. I fell to my knees over the commode, struggling to get my breath back. My friends looked at me but just then the bell rang for us to go back to class after lunch, and they ran out of the bathroom.

All I could do to help myself was to keep washing my face with the commode water. I was so scared. Later I thanked God that I hadn't got gonorrhea on my face from using the commode water.

Finally, after about fifteen minutes, I was able to get up off the floor and get myself together to go back to class. When I entered the classroom the teacher stood up and said, "Lucy, why are you coming to class so late?" I said, "I was in bathroom." She said, "What is that I smell? Have you been smoking?" I said, "I don't know," because I was afraid to lie to her. "I know you were smoking marijuana because I smell it and I see a burned spot on your uniform collar." Behind her back my girl friend held up her fist, and I knew that meant I better keep my mouth shut or there would be a big fight.

"Miss McCants, I found some weed on the bathroom floor and it was already lit, so I tried smoking it. It knocked me out so I had to stay in the bathroom until I could get myself together." She said, "I'm calling Miss Jenkins," and she knew my mother didn't play. I begged the teacher, "Please, please don't call my mother." She said, "I have to call her because you're on the road for a suspension." She went down the hall and called her.

In about ten minutes Mother arrived at school, wearing her wide brimmed sun hat full of holes and her raggedy apron and some tennis shoes. She came into the classroom and said, "Miss McCants, what's the matter up here?" My teacher said, "Lucy's been smoking." Mother said, "You know not to be smoking here at school. Lucy Jane, I'ma whup your ass." "You can't whup her in the classroom - take her to the bathroom." But my mother took me home. She took my clothes off me and whupped me naked. I promised her I would never smoke again, and I never have, not even a cigarette to this day. It was a good lesson that I learned.

I wish I could share that lesson with people who are facing the choice of trying drugs. But most people usually have to learn the hard way.

PROMISES FOR GRADUATES
by Lucy Ely

Promise yourself - to never forget God and your parents

The ones who made it possible for you to achieve thus far.

Promise yourself - to be so strong that nothing can disturb you from continuing your education. This is just the beginning. Your graduation from elementary Junior High through High School is the beginning for you to step higher.

Promise yourself - that nothing will disturb your mind. Believe you are going to be strong enough to talk health, happiness and prosperity, to every person you meet.

Promise yourself - you are going to make all your friends feel that there is something in them. Always look at the sunny side of everything and make your optimism come true. Think only of the best, to work for the best, and expect only the best.

Promise yourself - to be just as enthusiastic about the success of others as you are about your own self.

Promise yourself - to forget the mistakes of the past. Look at your mistakes not as a failure but as an experience and push on to greater achievements in the future.

Promise yourself - to wear a cheerful countenance at all times and give every living creature you meet a smile. To give so much time to improvement of yourself that you have no time to criticize others. To be too busy for worry, too noble for anger, too strong for fear and too happy to permit the presence of trouble.

Promise yourself always - to get an education. Education is an ongoing process. It never comes to conclusion.

Promise yourself - to climb the highest ladder to reach success.

You may be anything you desire to be. Above all, be the best.

Don't forget your parents and God.

EDUCATION
by Lucy Ely

E - is for everything you always wanted to be

D - is for doing all you can do

U - is for understanding. You need an understanding

C - is for calmness when your days get tough

A - is for asking for what you want or what you need

T - is for trust in yourself

I - is for interest in education and success

0 - is for ongoing to reach your goal

N - is for never, never forgetting God and your parents

GRADUATES- Promise yourself you are going to say Yes to an Education and say No to illegal street drugs.

A PRAYER OF THANKFULNESS TO GOD
by Lucy Ely

From a grateful heart, I am happy to say thank you God for the abundant blessings you have given to me. I am thankful for nourishing food, shelter, clothing, good health and the activities of My limbs.

I am grateful for the people in my life. They may be family members, friends, neighbors or people I come in contact with; each day of my life, I am thankful for every breath that I take, I breathe in the life and goodness of God.

My senses are blessed with the beauty of God's creation, they allow me to understand the beauty of the Seasons: Spring, Summer, Winter or Fall; yet during the seasons the weather, temperature and conditions change. Remember me, O Lord, to work in harmony with people around me, in my home, workplace or wherever I may be.

Thank You, Lord!

THINKING BACK OVER MY LIFE
by Lucy Ely

Looking back at my life twenty years ago, I thought I was going to die when I found out that I had a nodule on my trachea (windpipe), which caused me to have difficulty breathing. I was working and I had to support my three children. My husband and I were separated and I knew it was going to be difficult for me to take the time off from work to undergo surgery. I prayed and asked God for guidance and strength and to release my difficulty in breathing, because I was afraid that I would pass out, but deep down within, I knew that with my faith in God, I would be alright.

I woke up one morning and I prayed to God to take care of my children because I was going to have my surgery and I needed someone to care for them. God provided the way for my Mother to come to California to help me with the children.

My surgery went well. I had no recall or relapse. God had released me from all of my fears and doubts and now without any reservation, I know that without God I can do nothing. So, now I have learned to put away negative thinking into positive thoughts.

EASTER
by Lucy Ely

The Symbols of Easter

    1. The Cross
    2. The Eggs
    3. The Lamb
    5. The Lights - Words in Easter

E - Eggs new life to birth and nature.

A - Ask and it shall be given unto you.

S - Suffering, He died for us.

T - Tomb where He rose for us.

E - Eternal life for us.

R - Resurrection, Rejoice, Repent, Rise.

He is Risen! He is Risen!

Willie Francis

I am Willie Francis, a retired heavy construction administrator and a graduate of San Francisco State University. I spent four years in the U.S. Air Force and worked in Saudi Arabia for a number of years as a construction administrator building NGL's (Natural Gas Liquification Plants).

While working overseas I got to visit many countries in Africa and Asia. I am a member of the Write-On Writers' Workshop meeting at West Oakland Senior Center located at 18th and Adeline Street in West Oakland, CA.

RACE AND RACISM - IS IT A THING OF THE PAST OR IS IT STILL AMONG US?
by Willie Francis

African Americans today - in my humble opinion- are just as oppressed as they were before the passage of legislations making it illegal to discriminate against them because of their skin color. The 1964 Civil Rights Act has not solved the race problem. We are no longer confined to specific locations in this country. We can go pretty much where we please, as long as where we go and what we do conforms to what the system deems acceptable. Our bodies have been freed, but our minds remain trapped. We remain trapped in the belief that somehow we are not good enough.

When the schools were first integrated most of the white population became fearful that by sitting next to an African American child it would somehow prevent the white child from achieving his or her potential of being properly educated. However, they soon found that this was a myth. In fact, they found that not only would the white child continue to learn, but would learn at a much faster rate. The schools, being dominated by whites, developed school curriculum based upon the social economic background of the white group. This made the curriculum relevant to the white child. But for the black child, this approach had the effect of neutralizing, if not nullifying the black child's interest. The result being that the black child soon became disinterested. He could not see himself related to what was being taught. He soon became disengaged and looked for other things to hold his or her interest. This approach led to misbehavior and eventual excessive dropouts by the black students. Some may disagree with this analysis, but what I have found in my limited exposure to early childhood education is that if you are able to tie in the educational process at the school, with the socioeconomic development of the child outside of the school, the child will learn more quickly and retain what has been taught more effectively.

In the workplace today, blacks are still the last hired and the first fired. This will continue to be as long as we depend on others for our livelihood. We as black people seem to be antiwealth accumulation- but without it, we will not be able to control our destiny.

Ward Connolly, a former Regent at the University of California system and a black man, said that the California University system no longer needed an affirmative action program for black students - that further special consideration for them should be discontinued. Well, Mr. Connolly was wrong then and he is wrong now! You cannot undo the affects of cultural and economic racism in just a few years, when for hundreds of years, we were considered less than human. Blacks are graduating from the UC system today, but not nearly in the numbers that they should.

Whites, at this point and time in African American history, can not wholly be held responsible for our present plight. We, as a people, must assume our own destiny today. First of all, we must stop paying lip service to our blackness. We must feel that God did not make a mistake when he created us -that we have value, equal to, if not greater than any other human being. We must work hard to raise those values high so that others will see them as positive human attributes and want to come and share in our values and success. We can not continue to sit around waiting for others to do for us what we MUST do for ourselves.

The American system of education still favors the white child in most instances. The whites have the most money and therefore are able to say what curriculum should be in the classroom and how it shall be taught. Racism is not simply about the attitudes, dislikes, and motivation of individuals or individual acts of bigotry and discrimination.

Instead, racism refers to the way the American society as a whole is arranged and how the economic, educational, cultural, and social rewards of the American society are distributed.

Clarence Page, a noted television and newspaper colunmist, said: "Racism is a sensitive word. Americans avoid mentioning it, even when it is relevant .. .It is a sensitive word because it exposes so much, institutionally and personally. It is a Rorschach Word, a linguistic ink blot test. How you defme it reveals something important about you, how you see the world and your place in it." (1996)

The way that the American system looks at the social construct of blacks within the system is mostly negative. A young black boy walking along on a Florida street, in a middle-class neighborhood, is interfered with for no other reason than he is black. A young black boy was accosted and killed simply because somebody thought that he should not have been there. I suspect that had the young man been white this probably would not have happened.

In the school system of America, there is an alarming rate of young black boys in particular that are not finishing high school-47% in Oakland, CA alone. How can this be? Could it be that these young black people are not "gifted and black." I for one don't think for a moment that most of these young people cannot finish high school. The American system has failed them and the general black population is standing and sitting and letting this all happen!

I am a retired heavy construction administrator. I worked a great deal on the West Coast, particularly in California and the state of Washington. After working in the construction industry for a number of years, I found that many of the work projects that the company had going were highly unionized. That is, you had to belong to a union in order to work on a given project. I also noticed that the projects that we had, had very few blacks on them. Upon inquiring with the unions, particularly those with skilled craft people, as to why blacks were never sent out to the projects when requested, they told me that it was very difficult to get blacks to go through the necessary training programs in order to become qualified. They told me that when they put blacks into a training program, they would drop out as soon as they got their first check. This did not make any sense. The skilled crafts made the most money in the construction industry, yet no blacks wanted to participate? What I found out was that the unions would go into the worse areas of the black community and select the worse young people they could find and put them into a training program. This procedure is commonly called a "self fulfilling prophecy." That is, you make a statement about a particular situation, and then you go about creating conditions that would cause your prophecy to come about. Let's say it another way. You would say that blacks did not want to work, then you select young blacks that you had a pretty good idea would not stay in the program. Now you would write a letter to the Fair Employment Practice Commission. This letter would then justify your not having blacks in your training program. Therefore, when the contractor called the unions for workers, they would send out their friends, relatives, and the likes, and get away with it. Thanks to our American system of a fair and just chance to live and prosper.

When all is said and done, racism is still alive and well in the United States of America. It will only change when those who create legislation make sure that the ones that implement it, carrry it out fully to the extent of the law.

SOME PRINCIPAL PLAYERS AND MAKERS OF THE HARLEM RENAISSANCE
by Willie Francis

"The Harlem Renaissance was the most important period in twentieth century African American intellectual and cultural life", said Cary D. Wintz, a noted author.

The beginnings of the Harlem Renaissance was signaled by the movement of music, such as the blues and jazz, coming from such places as New Orleans, Memphis, St. Louis and Chicago, making its way to New York City, particularly Harlem. Blues singers like Mamie Smith and Bessie Smith became popularized. Jazz found its way to Harlem via a jazz player by the name of James Reese Europe in 1905. During World War I, Europe enlisted in the famed black Fifteenth Infantry Regiment known as the Harlem Hellfighters. He served overseas as a machine gun officer and band leader.

While overseas, Europe introduced jazz to the French and to Europeans in general. The new music took the European continent by storm. However, tragically, Europe was killed in 1919 by a deranged member of his own band in Boston.

In 1921 Eubie Blake and Nobel Sissie carried the soul of this new music to standing-room-only audiences on Broadway in New York in an all-black musical revue called *Shuffle Along*. Both the poet Langston Hughes and the influential poet and diplomat James Weldon Johnson saw the incredibly popular musical as a sign of the emerging Harlem Renaissance.

Another major event that marked the beginnings of the Renaissance was the 1924 Civic Club Dinner held to acknowledge the upsurge in black literary activities. In the early 1920's a series of unconnected literary events including Claude McKay's volume of poetry, Harlem Shadows (1922), Jean Toomer's novel Cane (1923), and the initial published works of other young black writers contributed to Harlem's emerging cultural life.

Charles S. Johnson, of the Urban League, organized the Civic Club Dinner in which the three major players in the literary Renaissance were brought together: the literary-political intelligentsia, white publishers and critics, and many black writers. Here are some of the major players and makers of the Harlem Renaissance:

1. James Weldon Johnson
A diplomat, poet, novelist, critic, and composer

2. Langston Hughes
Writer and poet

3. Claude McKay
Poet, novelist, and journalist

4. Alain Locke
Philosopher and literary critic

5. Scott Joplin
Ragtime composer and pianist

6. Billie Holiday
Vocalist and lyrist

7. Coleman Hawkins
Jazz tenor saxophonist

8. W.C. Handy
Blues musician

9. Ella Fitzzgerald
Singer and songwriter

10. James Reese Europe
Music administrator, conductor, and composer

11. Ralph Waldo Ellison
Novelist and essayist

12. Duke Ellington
Jazz musician, band leader, and composer

13. Paul Lawrence Dunbar
Author

14. W.E.B. Dubois
Scholar, writer, editor, and civil rights pioneer

15. Countee Cullan
Poet and playwright

16. A. Phillip Randolph
Labor organizer, editor, and civil rights activist

These are just a few of the many participants in the Harlem Renaissance.

WORKING IN SAUDI ARABIA
by Willie Francis

October 7, 2010

The Guy F. Atkinson Construction Company had just completed the San Pablo Dam Project in San Pablo, CA, for which I was an administrative manager, when they summoned me to the corporate office in South San Francisco. They told me that I had been chosen to go to Saudi Arabia to be a Field Manager for the company. I told them that before I accepted the appointment, I would have to discuss the matter with my wife. At the time, she was working for the Oakland Unified School District, as a high school counselor, and I did not feel that she would want to quit her position to go to a place where women were severely restricted. But, the money was good, and I felt that she probably would accept my going alone.

It took about a week for me to get everything in order before my departure. Of course, things like vaccinations, visa, wardrobe, and other items needed to be prepared. I was warned that because of the 125 degree temperature with no shade in sight and the sand's reflective base, synthetic clothing was not recommended, and if you did dare to wear synthetic clothing you would feel like you were being fried like an egg.

Before leaving for Saudi Arabia, I was told by some people in the corporate office that the Saudi's did not like black Americans: that I would have to be very careful when traveling around the country and if I broke any local laws, I would be arrested and jailed for a long time before the local Atkinson office would know where I was. On the contrary, however, I found that this was not the truth - not even close to the truth!

I was greeted at the Daharan Airport by an Atkinson company official who had been in the country for several months setting up the project. After securing my bags, we drove to the company's villa that doubled as a rest and relaxation retreat when our company's people came out of the desert for rest.

51

ARAMCO, a conglomerate of oil companies from America and Europe, worked for the Saudi government. Atkinson, however, worked for ARAMCO. ARAMCO occupied a large portion of desert somewhat west of the city of Daharan. It functioned like a city of its own, free to do whatever it wanted to, as long as it did not allow the common ordinary Saudi to participate. However, members of the Royal Saudi family came and went without restrictions, and did more revelry than the expatriates.

Soon I was working in the desert with a workforce of 20 men. Most of the men below the level of superintendent came from nearby countries like Pakistan, Somali, Sudan, Turkey, Yemen, and of course Saudi Arabia. However, most of the lower level supervisors had to be Saudis.

Atkinson, along with two other companies, had a contract with ARAMCO to build NGL's (Natural Gas Liquification Plants) in the desert. The NGL's captured the billions of gallons of natural gas that was released when crude oil was pumped from the ground. Natural gas is very volatile when released from the ground. This is why when you pass an oil well you will see a flame that burns continuously near where the crude oil is being extracted from the ground. The NGL is designed to capture the gas and put it under pressure, which causes it to liquefy. Once liquefied, the gas can be easily transported to market. The Saudis have one of the largest proven oil reserves in the world, which brings in billions of dollars each month. By building the NGL's, the Saudis doubled their profits, by capitalizing on the gas as a byproduct.

In driving across the desert, I began to interact with many of the nomads who traveled back and forth across the desert. I helped them by pulling their camels out of sand bogs with my four-wheel drive vehicle, giving them first-aid supplies, and most importantly, sharing precious water with them. Once I became more familiar with the local Saudis, we frequently had discussions on politics and comparative religion. To me, this was a good sign that the people, with whom I interacted accepted me and displayed comradeship.

It was about one year, however, before the local Saudi's invited me into their homes and introduced me to their families. They allowed me to talk with their wives and daughters without impunity. When invited to tea, young men dressed in traditional garb would serve us. One day I was summoned to report to the Emir Officer in Jubail. Jubail was a small town near where I was working in the desert, closer to the border of Kuwait. I just knew I was in trouble. But to my surprise, I was honored for the help I had given the nomads that I came across while working in the desert. I was made an honorary citizen and given a 22-carat gold ring and a key to the city.

I'd like to point out before I conclude concerning my brief stay in Saudi Arabia that the Emir and the Chief of Police of Jubail were both of African descent and they spoke of this heritage with great pride. Later, they urged me never to be ashamed of being who I was.

To the contrary of what had been said to me earlier, I had no problem blending into the culture and was given many privileges that were denied to many of my colleagues. This caused much resentment with ex-patriots, and they accused me of "going native". I did not mind the accusation because it helped me to execute my duties with fewer problems. When my assignment was over, the project director asked me if I'd like to stay on. Four years was long enough for me, being away from home and my family. Two weeks later, I was on a plane, back to the U.S.A. The experience was great, but there is nothing like being back home!

ODE TO JACKSON ROYSTER
by Willie Francis

Jack Royster was a quiet person. He would sit at our table saying very little unless asked several times to speak. Upon urging, Jack would sift through a large stack of unorganized papers and come up with an amazing taste of history that for most people had long been forgotten, or better yet, never known.

He spoke of the many prize fighters of the past who got their start here in Oakland. Prizefighters, such as Sugar Ray Robinson and Sugar Ray Leonard, just to name a few. He brought back the Black Life that existed along Seventh Street in West Oakland. He spoke of the many night clubs that found life there, with all the jazz and blues bands playing the clubs.

Jack was full of Black History. History that he researched and recorded on paper and in his mind. He was born in West Oakland in 1945, and passed away sometime in early March, 2014. I wish Jack well in his afterlife, for he left us far too soon!

NATHANIEL H. FRANCIS - MY GRANDSON
WHAT HE SAID TO ME ONE DAY
by Willie Francis

I was sitting at the dining room table one evening, trying very hard to come up with something meaningful to write about. My grandson, who was 7 years at the time, was playing on the floor next to me when suddenly he stood up and said, " Grandpa, what are you doing?" I replied, haltingly, that I was trying to come up with something to write about. He replied, "Grandpa, if you can't think of anything to say, write about me!" I said, "Oh?" and was taken aback by his interest. "What can I say about you?" I replied. He looked at me for a few minutes, then said this:

My Family is sweet, loving, and care very much for me. They buy me stuff that I like, such as Wii and Nintendo DS with lots of games. They take me on vacations that are fun. My Mom loves me and I love her back. No one can stand between our love. The most I love about her is that she never changes. I like the way she is. My Grandpa is nice also. He cares for me, feeds me, and he takes me where I want to go. He is trying to make me more responsible. He likes the way I am and I like the way he is. Even though sometimes he is disappointed in me - he still loves me and I still love him. My Grandma appreciates me too. Sometimes I help my Grandma with her needs, like waking her up to tell her that her breakfast is ready. No matter what happens, I will still love her.

My cousins Tracie, Sean, and Aaron are the best. One time my cousin Aaron took me to a basketball game. He let me play with his band members at the basketball game. He didn't get mad at me when I accidentally dropped and broke a bowl in the kitchen. My cousin Sean is one and a half years old. When I play with him he laughs and seems like he's having a good time. My cousin Tracie takes me places that I've never been before, like the Discovery Museum in Washington, D.C. One time she took me to a children's fun place. There were mazes that you had to figure out how to get through. We played indoor hockey, basketball, and laser tag. I had so much fun, I hope Mom lets me go back to Washington, D.C., soon.

Clotile
Sanford-Hunt

After working for AT&T for 30 years, I retired
to pursue my lifelong dream of becoming a
teacher. It wasn't until I joined the Creative
Writing Workshop at the West Oakland Senior
Center that I realized my passion for the written
word. Through poetry, I am able to slay my
demons and nurture my dreams. I discovered
that writing helps me stay grounded and gives
me strength to endure the good as well as the
bad.

FIRST BORN
by Clotile Sanford-Hunt

Let's have a baby, we both agreed.
Then how come the only one getting fat is me?
Swollen feet and hunger pains
No one told me about the weight I'd gain.
The doctor said "we're doing fine."
Just a warning, nine months is a long time.
One more push and you were here
All wrinkles and screams, music to my ears.
Now you are grown and have moved away,
But I will always remember that day
Filled with pain and joy,
Of the birth of my first baby boy.

FOREVER FRIENDS
by Clotile Sanford-Hunt

Come run with me
through the sand laughing and giggling feeling free,
the cold water of the ocean lapping at our legs
not caring just having a wonderful time!

Come dance with me
the night club's hot, we got our working girl shoes and hutchie
mama dresses on
ready to set the town on fire!

Come sit with me
you know on that old rickety swing we put up years ago
sitting, talking, laughing, sharing things,
secrets,
solving world peace over cookies and tea

Come walk with me
Slowly, picking our steps, reminiscing about the good old days
wondering where that guy was that could kiss so well
hey, you married him didn't you?
Remembering yesterday

Come lie with me
It's time to go
we both know we got more to do but our bodies are so tired we can't
but it's okay

Come fly with me
up to the clouds hand in hand laughing and giggling
memories of the past slipping away
anxious for our new unknown journey

FULL CIRCLE
(SIX WORD STORY)
by Clotile Sanford-Hunt

Cancer, the essences of her life vaporized.

LENNY MAE:
A MONOLOGUE
by Clotile Sanford-Hunt

My name is Lenny May and I'm from Memphis, Tennessee. I was supposed to be named after my aunts Leanora and Margret, but my mother couldn't spell Leanora so she called me Lennie, but spelled it like Penny only with an L instead of a P. When I asked her why she didn't name me Margaret, she said, "Margaret was a big fat woman with breasts down to her stomach and her stomach hung down to her knees and she didn't want me to grow up to look like her, so she named me May instead."

Now 1 am a woman for all seasons and every season has a reason. The reason for Fall, where the sycamore leaves turn orange, is Detroit City. I loved Detroit and visiting my cousin Jill. Mostly I loved Jill's neighbor, Slick Willie. Slick Willie and his twin brother Candyman lived next door to Jill. Candyman's real name was Bernard, but we called him Candyman because he always gave the girl he was going to walk home a piece of peppermint candy. If a girl refused the candy, he would walk away from her and find someone else to give it to. I asked him about the candy and he said that he gave them a piece of candy because he refused to kiss a girl with stinky breath. Slick Willie's real name was Joseph, but he felt that it was too biblical so he insisted that everyone call him Willie. Willie had a big Cadillac and worked at the radio station as a DJ. I called him Slick Willie because he could slick talk any girl he saw into visiting the back seat of his car. Boy, we made some good music in that back seat! I don't visit Detroit any more because Willie died a while back. He was sneaking around with Junebug's wife Penelope. One night Junebug came home early and caught them in bed butt-necked and stabbed them with a pair of scissors. At the trial, he pleaded guilty and then dropped dead of a heart attack.

Springtime means a trip to Memphis. I love visiting my daughter and nephew, but sometimes they can get on my nerves. Another reason for visiting Memphis is Lumberjack, the carpenter. Jack's real

61

name is Peter, but I think walking around calling a grown man Peter sounds sexually suggestive, so I call him Lumberjack because he really knows how to use his "tools." Once when I was in Memphis, I had a late date with Jack, so while I was taking a nap my nephew, Eddie, decided he would take his wife to the movies and leave his bad kids with me. His older daughter, Danni, was coming over around 10:00 to spend the night so they figured they could leave, and since I was there, the younger kids wouldn't be alone. They told them to wake me up if anything was wrong. I didn't tell them about my date because they are too nosey. I woke up about 10:00 when I heard Danni come in. I called my cab and left. The next morning as the cab pulled up to the house, Eddie came running out of the house shouting, "Where have you been all night? We were worried!" I just walked past him and put my overnight bag in the room. He kept on shouting, "We got up and you had not made coffee and biscuits like you usually do, so I thought you were sleeping late. When I listened at the door I could hear your radio playing and was shocked to find an empty bed. I called Mama and Uncle Joe, I even called Aunt Mattie. No one had heard from you so I was about to call the police." He followed me into the kitchen, repeating "Where were you?" Finally I turned around and said, "I was with my boyfriend, nosey!" He walked away, shaking his head and laughing.

I don't travel anymore because my knees are bad. I do have a boyfriend. His name is Old Joe. He is the only thing I let in my house that is old. I told my kids a long time ago that I don't want anything old around me except old money. I have a new house, new car, even new furniture. 1 am getting tired of Joe because he's lazy and expects me to take his wife's place. Joe's wife died last year. The doctors said her body just wore out from waiting on Joe hand and foot. He's not going to do that to me. He eats too much greasy food and way too much candy. He'll get diabetes if he doesn't watch out. He never wants to go anywhere except to church and he is too boring for me, so I'm going to kick him to the curb and latch on to someone who doesn't need a pillow to prop them up.

Last year for my 100th birthday and my children gave me a party. There were over 100 people there. All of them relatives! We had all kinds of food and drinks. I even got up and danced! I got lots of new clothes and enough money to put a down payment on a Chevy. Of course I would have to hire me a nice young man to drive me around.

MEMORIES
by Clotile Sanford-Hunt

Let's throw a party old school style
Let's dance and sing to the music

Sipping wine and feeling loose
Dancing slow cheek to cheek
Holding each other close
Making love on the dance floor
Having the time of our life

Whispered secrets and silly lies
Sneaking a forbidden kiss
Touching and caressing
Sweating and breathing hard

Loss of memory and an aching head
Not wanting to forget the ecstasy
Of kissing and fumbling exhausted and happy
Not looking forward to the giggles and incriminating stares
Conflicted feeling of guilt and satisfaction

Just feeling alive and free

Let's throw a party old school style

Let's drink and dance the night away

Reliving our youth and making these the good days

MOTHERHOOD
by Clotile Sanford-Hunt

The smell of dirty diapers filling the room like outhouses
in the summer heat
Bottles of formula boiling in large metal pots sterilizing the contents
White baby powder covering everything like dust in an abandoned house
Morning feeding signals the sun to begin its journey through the day
Endlessly pacing the floor at midnight making shushing sounds
like white noise

Chasing those precious 15 minutes of sleep and not realizing
you have caught them
Spending endless hours washing small pieces of cloths
like the women at the river
Constantly cleaning the same area like a person
with OCD needing medication
Duplicating every move like a robot hoping for rest unattainable

Looking into the eyes of my clone and feeling the Godlike power
of reproducing myself
Swallowing tiny hands in mine and knowing I am immortal,
omnipotent
Hearing gurgling sounds like a mountain spring telling me
I am loved unconditionally
Just as Fall acquiesces to Winter, my power of immortality waned
No longer the Sun with the planets revolving in their own
designated paths around me
Usurped by the gravitational pull of the universe
ruled by sex, drugs and technology
My clone transmuted into a being of independent thought
and rebellion

Reversal of seasons like the return of the salmon
to spawn marks the full circle

No longer has the center, a new star been discovered illuminating
the heavens

ODE TO A LITTERBOX
by Clotile Sanford-Hunt

A square plastic box, always square never round, rectangular or cone shaped. A square to keep the contents in check and controlled. The box is covered with an open-ended dome to shield from unknowing eyes the true contents, ugly and fowl smelling. Sparkling blue crystals evenly cover the bottom giving the illusion of precious gems.

A stream of self-doubt pollutes the sparkling gems causing them to clump together, dimming their brilliance. The clumps are quickly covered in a shroud of bright, shiny crystals putting on the facade of newness. The piling on of self loathing and despair makes what was once breathtaking into a stench that makes you hold your breath. Falling deeper into hopelessness they are buried in the box to mask the odors and revolting sight. Routinely the graduals are removed and fresh ones take their place giving the impression of cleansing and renewal. The replacements will perform the task only to come to the same fate as their predecessor's, a short existence in a square plastic box.

EMBERS OF A FIRE
by Clotile Sanford-Hunt

Childhood memories are like embers of a fire
Banked for the night so it won't burn out
Some of the coals have turned to ash, but
Others wait quietly for the stroke of the poker.

Recalling the past is like eating at a smorgasbord
As you walk around the counter you pile food on your plate
Your mouth waters with anticipation,
Romanced by the smells,
Your stomach churns like an anxious lover's.

Revived by the smell of homemade bread fresh from the oven.
Hearing your favorite song played on the radio and your toes
begin to ache because the cute boy didn't know how to dance.
Touching your lips and feeling your first stolen kiss.
A sharp pain in your heart when an ambulance roars past
and death came through your door.

Memories give us joy and remind us of loss
They remind us of who we were and who we want to be
They are the glue that keeps us strong and the unraveling of the
tapestry of life that makes us weak.

LAST JOURNEY
by Clotile Sanford-Hunt

Today a friend has gone away, no pills to take or debts to pay.

No more rotting liver or uncontrollable drinking binges.
No more living in anger and despising the fear
No more making excuses and displacing the blame.
No more hurting the ones who try to hold you near.

No more avoiding mirrors to hide from the image
through the brown haze.
No more lying on cold floors retching
No more waiting for the waves of pain to subside
Each day of loathing all the same

Surrendering to the grim reaper and yearning for rest
He can smell his burning flesh as death his soul singes.
He now takes the dreaded journey down a mysterious road
Not caring where it leads, just hoping for an escape

SECRET LOVE
by Clotile Sanford-Hunt

Sneaking down the alley, keeping out of sight
Heart pounding, knowing he is waiting giving me a fright.
So excited to be seeing him and knowing it's a sin.
But when his lips touch mine the world begins to spin.

Sneaking down the alley and climbing up the stairs
So afraid someone will hear us avoiding all the glares
Sneaking down the alley laughing all the way,
If they could see us what would our grandchildren say?

Born in Florida and raised in New Jersey, Jennifer is currently the director of the Downtown Oakland Senior Center. She also teaches English, Composition, and Public Speaking at the College of Alameda and at the Allen Temple Leadership Institute in Oakland.

In 2007 she published her first book of poetry, Turning My Face to the Sun, and in 2013 she published And Then I Cried, an anthology of her poetry and short stories. She is a regular writer of Christian Education and Sunday School Teacher's materials for Urban Ministries, Inc. Her own poetry, essays, and short stories have been published in a number of journals, anthologies, and periodicals both locally and nationally. Jennifer is a graduate of Mills College, and holds a BA and an MA in English. Jennifer is an avid reader and enjoys travelling. She is a resident of Oakland, and the proud mother of one child, Lauren Justine.

FLYING WITH BIG MOMMA
by Jennifer D. King

The '68 Buick taxis from the runway.
　The house disappears
　　　　from view
　　Big Momma backs up— turns her chariot.
　　Cashmere Bouquet wafting from the pilot's breasts
　　　　mingle with Sister's Juicy Fruit in the back seat.

Cleared for take-off
　　　Big Momma jets
　　　　　　onto the highway.
　　Tons of steel and chrome
　　　　　go hurling down the asphalt
　　spewing dust
　　　　　smashing snakes.
　　Steady pressure on the accelerator connect the highway
dividing lines.
At Her command
　　telephone poles become neatly ordered rows of crosses
　　　　　　as we fly
　　　　　　　down
　　　　　　　　the highway.
60—She slips
　　　behind
　　　　　careens past
　　a log-hauling semi—oblivious to her wide-eyed passengers,
clutching hot vinyl seats.
Teeth clench as Big Momma propels the car
　　　　　across the Chattahoochee Bridge.
75 —She shares
gory details
a white man wrapped his speeding pick-up
　　　　　　　around
　　　　　　　　unyielding Spanish moss.

85— She soars
                    past the hospital
                              that does not admit colored people.
90—Big Momma begins her medley of flying hymns .
        Some glad morning when this life is over
                              I'll fly away ...
95—Sister hyperventilating —
sucking her thumb at the same time;
        my bladder surrenders.
Big Momma is still   flying
                    and singing
                              about heaven
                                        and blood
                                                  and Jesus.

Her Jesus—Sister and I decide
must be the patron saint of flying grandmothers.

GRATEFUL
by Jennifer D. King

Grateful for a mother that hugged and held me
Kissed and scolded
Had no problem embarrassing me in front of my friends
Because they didn't love me
Like she loved me.

Grateful for a father who encouraged and cheered
and spanked and yelled
who had no problem walking into the den in his boxer shorts
just cause "it's his damned house!"
and
because he loves me more
than the knucklehead who's trying to feel me up
on the sofa.

Grateful for the sister who teaches me how to slow dance
put on eye shadow
and hide a hickey with foundation
who will—if provoked—beat me down
And who will beat down anyone who threatens to beat me down
Because she loves me more than the school bully

Grateful for the brother who wore orthopedic shoes
until he was three
who ate paper money
who wrapped a towel around his shoulders
called it a cape—declared he was Superman

and leaped from the roof of the garage
who would never listen to me
would not obey me
until he turned 20
and began to hear
voices
that no one else could hear
then
he listened to me
because he knew
that I loved him more
than the people who knew he was crazy

Doris M. Phelps

I am the mother of one adult son, and a native of Oakland, California. A graduate of Mills College, I love to travel and read.

Joyous days of experiencing the emotions written words evoke, I write poems and stories exploring and expanding life's adventures creatively.

As I enter this new chapter of my life, I thank God for the journey and hope you enjoy my works.

THE CB RADIO
by Doris M. Phelps

Up and down the red dirt road my cousins and I would toss rocks, giggle and chase each other from house to house. You could see the smoke from the chimneys of the three houses on the no-name road that was Papa's property, left to my great grandfather and passed down through generations.

The small Louisiana town wasn't even listed on the road maps back then in the 1950's, and there weren't any street signs like back home on the corners.

Auntie would yell, "Stay on the road and don't cross the fields, might come across a snake out there." "Yes ma'am," we answered.

Crackle, pop, buzzzzzzzzzzzzzzzzzz. That's the sound of the strange radio in my aunt's bedroom.

"Cruiser One here comin at yah," stated the voice of a strange man. My cousin would giggle and say, "There he goes again."

All of my relatives had radios you could talk to each other on. I was amazed at this. There were no antennas or even numbers for the stations. How did they know who was who? We had little radios that fit in the palm of your hand at home in different colors; mine was pink. My Dad had a bigger one, no one could touch, but he only listened to music, the ball games and the fights at home.

"Auntie, what kind of radio is that?" I asked. "Hush, now girl, it's a CB, got to hear what's goin on," she stated. "Yawl ain't got no CB's," my cousin whispered. "No," I answered.

Gabbing me by the arm, she pulled me across the room. "Everybody down here got one, so's you can find out what the white forks is doing." "Huh," I said. "Girl, when the white folks stops us on the road or the Night Riders is out we got to know. Listen, that's a code they up by the church," she whispered. "What they doing?" I asked. "Hush up now," my aunt said, "Old possums by the Cross." I heard another voice come over the CB radio. My aunt yelled, "Yawl go on in the bedroom and turn out them lights."

78

We ran in the room and my cousin said, "Get down by me on the floor, got to wait and see what gone happen next."

After a while I heard my uncle's big red truck he drove with the back full of lumber come in the yard. It was a long time before he came in the house.

"Everything's all right; they headed on up the back road towards town," I heard him tell my aunt.

"What do they want?" I whispered to my cousin. "Don't know, but last week they set a fire and all the mens is on call. We can't let them burn our houses. Them some mean white men. Mamas got a big gun if they show up outside."

That night I couldn't sleep and listened to the CB radio and my aunt and uncle's voices in the dark each time a new message came in.

I know we got some mean white folks at home too, I thought. One day we were shopping and a white lady said, "Don't know why they let all these niggas come in these stores." Her kids started laughing. Mama just held my hand tight and we walked away. She told us to never say that mean word or we would get a whipping.

The next morning I asked my aunt if I could call my mama. I wanted to go home. I guess she could see the fear in my face. "Baby, your mama gone call us on Saturday, just like last week. Now hand me that pan on the stove and set the table for me."

I jumped at the sound of the CB radio. "Breaker, breaker, this is the Lone Ranger." "Ain't nothing to be afraid of, just your uncle telling he on his way home to eat." She smiled and patted me on the head. While setting the table my aunt said, "You know every-one down here doesn't have a telephone, so the CB radio is a way for us to keep in touch. When your uncles and your grandpa are out in the woods cutting logs we need a way to find out if there's been an accident so we can get them help. Same thing when the roads are flooded and muddy after a hard rain and someone gets stuck on the side of the road or there's a bad accident. Yah, we done had a few bad run-ins with some of the Night Riders, so it's important that we memorize the CB radio codes for trouble and keep our ears open at all times. Do you understand?"

"Yes," I stammered.

 "So, don't be afraid chile, it's just our way of communicating down here. You'll get used to it just like we did. Yawl's daddy gone get one for yawl's car, when he comes to take yawl home."

I smiled.

FOUNDERS DAY
by Doris M. Phelps

Sharon Hayes slammed on her brakes again. "Lord I got about one fourth of a mile before I reach my exit. Can you believe this? Two fender benders, a motor cycle cutting off a tour bus, some nut giving the finger after zooming across three lanes and now folks screaming and cursing all over the place. I don't know why I let Jolene talk me into joining this church way across town. This traffic is enough to make anyone lose their religion." She pounded the steering wheel with frustration. "Thank you, Lord," she shouted as she took her exit off the highway.

Sharon smiled as she approached the Zion Baptist Church parking lot. She sped into a slot and cut off her engine. Thanks to commute traffic she was always running late for the young women's study group.

"Woman, you got to slow down!" Deacon Zander Banks yelled, approaching her as she slid out the car, slammed the door and hit her alarm button. There he was again, a gorgeous chocolate Adonis who stood before her with a smile that made her legs wobble. She was determined to keep her cool but let out a small chuckle. He had been assigned to the circle as Bible instructor. Each week he greeted her with a smile that could melt her insides and made her eyes so dreamy they captured you in a grip that stopped you in your tracks.

"Evening, Deacon," she whispered, turning to walk toward the back door.

"Evening, Ms. Hayes, late again I see," Zander chuckled, getting a sneak peak at her bottom before catching up and opening the door for her. One of these days he was going to invite her to coffee he thought.

"Traffic was a bear like always," she responded, walking swiftly toward the classroom.

"Glad you could make it." He tilted his head as they entered the room and shut the door behind them.

Sliding into the nearest vacant chair she pulled out her Bible, plastered on a shy smile, and peered around the room at the ladies gathered. She noticed Jolene giving her a thumbs up from the back of the room.

Sandra Hill, the circle president, approached the podium. "Ladies, the pastor has asked that we organize this year's Founders Day celebration. Usually dinner is served in the parking lot. Hopefully we can use the dining hall and get out of that blazing sun. Normally they don't have a program, but I was thinking perhaps this year we could do something to showcase our church families and include musical selections, and maybe praise dancing from the youth. I'd like volunteers for committee chairpersons. You don't all have to raise your hands at once." She giggled as she distributed the outline she'd composed, including the list of committees. "Think it over and give me a call," she continued. "At next month's meeting let's try to have a list of committee members as well as a list of suggestions we can present to the pastor. The good Deacon has waived our regular study for tonight in an effort for us to get started. We have three months to get organized and submit a budget, which he will present to the Executive Board. " Sharon began describing the duties of each committee.

Deacon Banks approached the podium. "Good evening ladies, I'd like to request Sister Jolene to work with me on the History Committee; it has been brought to my attention that it needs to be updated and I could use her clerical skills. I'd also like to request any family artifacts that the members would like to display to be directed to me and I'm soliciting the Youth Department to assist with setting up the displays and making signs. That's all I have for tonight." Every eye followed his long legs and strong muscles as he made his way to his seat.

One hour later the ladies closed out the meeting and headed for the parking lot.

"Hey, Ms. lately come late, why don't I ever see you at Sunday services?" Zander had finally decided it was time he got to know something about this woman who creeps into his dreams.

"Well, when I first joined I worked mostly every Sunday. Sister Jolene encouraged me to come to the circle to meet some of the other women. So here I am." Sharon spoke softly.

"What about now?" Xavier cocked his head and a smile spread across his handsome face.

Sharon blushed, thinking to herself, is he really trying to flirt with me? "Old habits die hard," she whispered.

"Well, drive safely." He slowly turned and headed for his own vehicle across the lot. "Her innocent gray eyes. Her simple little smile. I can't believe how beautiful you are. Man you have lost it," he whispered to himself in the night air.

Chapter 2

Three evenings later Sharon lounged on her two sectional sofa, enjoying a cup of coffee. Looking across the room at her sixty-inch television she laughed at the answers the Family Feud guest once again got wrong. A small breeze blowing through the window gave a slight rise to the customized curtains she had ordered on line. She'd spent an entire day shopping for the right color to add cheer and brightness to her small, two-bedroom home. When she'd purchased this house it was a step toward moving on with her life. Staying in the old neighborhood was depressing. She wanted to step out each morning to smiling neighbors who knew nothing about her past. Before moving to Berkeley and relocating from her parent's home she was restless. The last few years had been stressful and she had made numerous adjustments. Slowly she was reclaiming her life and her prayers were being answered. Switching the channel to watch the nightly news her phone rang. She reached over to pick up the receiver and said, "Hello."

"Hello to you too, girlfriend. What's up with you and the good deacon?" Jolene inquired.

"I should be asking you that," Sharon countered.

"Woman, every time you two enter the room eyes get to rolling," Jolene bellowed.

"I can't imagine why," Sharon stated.

"Honey, you have been alone too long. If you can't see and feel vibes from a man that's interested in you, something is seriously wrong," Jolene laughed.

"Jolene, we were simply walking in from the parking lot, girl. It's no big deal, he's usually patrolling the lot when I arrive."

"Oh, he's patrolling all right, your cute little behind. You should see the smile on that handsome face watching you till you sit down. A couple of the good sistah's have been checking it out too. I heard a few in the ladies restroom saying, 'we got something for that chocolate thunder.' Seems like he's been rejecting a few invites to Sunday dinner. They didn't know I was in the far stall, when one of them inquired if he was gay and another politely corrected her and gave them the four one-one. She stated he moved here after a bad divorce." Jolene continued to rattle on and on.

"Well, I saw a few frowns and jaws drop when he asked you to be on his committee," Sharon piped up, giggling.

"Now, you know I got a man, so when he calls for a meeting be ready to have my back. James is cool and all, but I don't trust myself with that hunk of a man. Course now, this is a good opportunity for you to get to know him." Jolene's eyes widened as she spoke.

"Jolene, I don't know about this." Sharon rolled her eyes upward.

"Come on girl, you're a writer, we could use your input. Why don't you come to church this Sunday and we can go out to dinner afterward and go over the draft he's bringing to me."

Jolene continued to press.

"I'll give you a call and let you know Saturday." With that said, Sharon hung up, shaking her head. She wouldn't get a wink of sleep tonight dreaming about how the Deacon's strong arms would feel holding her all night. *I wonder what he looks like when he awakes in the morning.*

Jolene smiled as she hung up. Her old friend was beginning to soften up a little. She remembered a few years ago when she returned to town and stayed in her parent's old house. Unfortunately, she was alone with both parents gone and then losing her only sibling. Growing up their families had been close and after their death she had encouraged her brother to give up his apartment and live in the family home which she had remodeled for her mother following her dad's death. She recalled shopping with the two of them and the joyous times they'd shared. Sharon had finally sold one of her novels and it had hit the top-10 selling list. Sharon was on top of the world until she discovered her cheating husband had been having an affair with their neighbor's daughter. His quarterly business trips had been secret rendezvous to meet up with the girl near her college campus. After her graduation they ran off together and he mailed her divorce papers. The girl's parents didn't blame her: however, she just couldn't face them day after day. Her brother's unexpected death was a test of her faith.

Chapter 3

Zander slammed the front door of his two-story Spanish-style condo and marched over to plop down on his couch. "Why do these crazy things keep happening to me?" he shouted. He felt like his head was about to explode. This day had kicked off with his mom phoning at 6:00 this morning to say how cute his ex-fiancé had looked at the supermarket yesterday. The woman was a demon in disguise. All she ever did was lie, lie, lie. But his saint of a mother, Doralee Knight, kept encouraging him to forgive and forget. Lord, all she's concerned about is dying and having no grandchildren to brag about to her circle sisters at church before she's put six feet under.

By noon he'd received two calls from school counselors about two of his boys. Opening the boys home had been his dream. He had grown up without his father, Nehemiah Knight, who had died at age 25 in a car accident. His mother, whom he adored, had done her best to raise her boy child. He had been a Boy Scout, Little League player, member of the neighborhood Boys and Girls Club, church youth usher, and anything else she thought would provide her son with male contact and guidance. His grandfather, Moses, and uncles had kept him busy fishing, cleaning the yards, going to car shows and whatever they felt was macho. He'd made a few bad choices along the way, but today's world offered too many distractions and not enough positive guidance. His boys were referred by several friends, all social workers, who like him wanted to steer them in the right direction, teach them to trust and make goals for themselves.

"Why do youth always let the actions of others cloud their judgment and sense of right and wrong? These kids have got to learn to control themselves and stop lashing out without analyzing the outcome of things. We talk about there will be consequences for their actions all the time," he yelled out loud.

Bam, bam, baaaaaaaaaaaam, "Hey man you in there?" The robust voice of his longtime friend, Jesse Anderson, could be heard outside his door. "Man, I don't know who was chasing your behind that you forget to close your car door, else I just disturbed a robber from ripping you off when I rolled up. Come on and open up before sweet little Mrs. Crabcake calls the police again." He continued banging on the door.

"Wow, what truck ran over you? You had a bad day, huh?" The look on his friend's face spelled trouble. He'd seen this expression many times over the years. Working with the boys home was truly a challenge. Today's teens had problems that could make a man weep. Broken homes, drug addiction, absentee parents, homelessness and abuse were a constant that created a bunch of disturbed and violent kids striking out against the world.

"Man, these kids are off the hook. How many times have I told them fighting doesn't solve anything. We try to remove them from abusive environments and show them a different way, using their minds instead of their fists, but they keep reverting back. Hell, what's next?" Xavier rubbed his bald head and took a gulp from the juice he'd poured prior to answering the door.

"Hey, I dropped by the house and Howard said you'd taken off for the day. He kind of filled me in on what's going on with Jamir and Donte. I figured you'd taken refuge here. Man, you're the best thing that could happen to those kids, but don't forget they're with you because of what they've gone through. You've dedicated the past five years to helping wayward boys, and you're the only one I know who's got the patience and a few good results," Jessie stated.

"Man, I don't feel like talking about it right now. You want something? Help yourself." He pointed to the juice bottle on the table.

"What we both need is a cold beer. Let's go to the Man Hole and down a few." Jessie eyed his friend. You know, since you stopped drinking and went on strike from the ladies you're quite the bear. Frustration can be a mean thang man. Don't you think it's time you started living again. Come on, all this stress can kill a brother. Jessie smiled, shaking his head. His old friend had sworn off women after opening the Boys Home. He wanted to be an example for his boys and teach them to respect women, but after he'd discovered his woman was not what she appeared to be it had left a bitter taste where women were concerned. "Looks like you either need a cold shower or a beer."

"Come on man, give me a break. Besides I need to go over to the house and hold a meeting. My boys may be a challenge but I can't give up on them and I refuse to let them be gobbled up by the streets. We made it out the projects and so can they. Plus I've got to talk to them about the Founders Day program." Zander threw up his hands.

"You better know it man, but times weren't this bad. I'm a grown man and I'm scared to walk through those projects. All the graffiti and trash, not to mention the guns, it's insane." Jessie let out a deep breath. "Hey, we had pride in where we lived. You never saw trash anywhere and we respected our mamas not to mention we were scared to death of them. Plus we wanted better and believed we could make it. Man these kids don't have the parents we did. Most of their moms are strung out and who knows what happened to the fathers. So many in jail and the others just don't care." Jessie shook his head. "Well, in case you didn't notice I brought food, so let's chow down and you can fill me in on your new duties." Jessie brought the food to the table and opened the bag from their favorite Chinese restaurant.

"Thanks man, I'm going to need your help with the updating of the church's history. I know Moms has programs dating back fifty years in that trunk of hers. Why don't you see if we can set up a Saturday morning to go over them and try to see what we can find. " Zander took a gulp of juice and grabbed a fork to dig in to his favorite sweet and sour chicken dish.

"Do you remember Mrs. Withers? She used to teach the children's Sunday School Class. I know she's got plenty of old photos and probably more information than my Mom. I'll ask Mom to check and see if we pay her a little visit. If we let her know what we're looking for she'll be glad to help, man. Plus it'll give me a chance to see that sexy daughter, De Anna. That sweet little girl grew up to be a real looker. She's got curves in all the right places and when she sash shays down the aisle those hips hypnotize, yeeeeeeeah. " Jessie shouted and pumped his fist in the air.

Chapter 4

"Afternoon, Pastor," the small group standing in the parking lot greeted.

"Good afternoon to you all," he greeted. Rev. Timothy Jones was delighted to see this group assembled together. This was his third year serving as senior pastor of the Zion Baptist Church. He was wearing his clergy robe, a gift from the Deacon Board, presented to him at last year's Founders Day celebration. He wasn't quite as tall as the young men surrounding him, but he was proud of the respect they had shown him since his arrival at the church. He scratched his balding head and smiled that winning smile that illuminated his cocoa-colored face, revealing perfect white teeth. "Sisters and Brothers, I am truly impressed with the way you took charge of the Founders Day activities. Oh, there were a few complaints in the beginning, but I suggested that they give you a chance. I saw untapped potential and was confident in all your skills. Sister Sharon, it's nice to see you at the morning services, and your work with the youth is to be commended. Deacon Zander has his hands full but your zeal and artistic talents have been a winning factor with the youth. I've even noticed a few more parents in attendance," said Rev. Jones.

"Thank you, pastor, I've enjoyed myself as well," Susan answered.

"Sister Jolene, you and Brother Jessie here, you've done a wonderful job working with the seniors, compiling the history through photos, not to mention the great artifact displays. I can't tell you how many phone calls and compliments I've received on your behalf. The members are just buzzing about all of your work. I know that when great minds get together we will achieve great things. I didn't see Sister De Anna this morning but you bet I'll give her a call and thank her and her mother for their input."

"Pastor Jones, we were proud to do all we could. I must say things are coming together better than we expected." Jessie smiled and shook the pastor's hand.

"Well, the big day is almost here and I'm quite excited. Thank you all again for your hard work." He gave them all a hug and proceeded to his office.

"Sounds like we've earned a good hot meal everybody. Sandra and Jolene, how about you join Jessie and me for dinner at the Red Lobster? I need to get the boys home and settled but could meet you around five o'clock if that sounds good." Zander smiled that killer smile as he looked into Sharon's eyes.

"You paying, I'm coming," Jessie replied laughing. "I'll even call De Ann and see if she's game."

"Sounds like a deal to me: Sharon and I will meet you there."
Jolene grabbed Sharon by the hand and started walking and
waving before she could back out. "Don't look back now but I
think his smile just got bigger," Jolene giggled.

Zander's hormone level was soaring and he'd never even kissed
her. She was beautiful and he'd waited over a year for this day.

Chapter 5

"Honestly, I don't know what I'm going to do with you." Sharon
stood at her door barking at Jolene at precisely four o'clock.

"Come on woman, you've got a date with a gorgeous man, and my
palate has one with a juicy lobster. Now where is that stunning
brown pant suit you just bought? Let that hair down and work it
girl." Jolene headed for the bedroom, pushing Sharon aside.

"I don't know about this, Jolene." Sharon stood in the doorway
pondering if this was a good idea.

"Listen, for the past six months you've denied yourself this man's
company and I want to know why. He's great on the eyes, has a
stable job, goes to church and has it bad for you, girlfriend. Now
from what I can tell he's as scared as you are, honey. Don't you
dare pass up this opportunity. Just take it slow, but you deserve
to be happy just like the rest of us. I'm sick of those floozies at
church throwing themselves at your man." Jolene softly patted
her hand.

"But he's not my man," Sharon said nervously.

"Maybe you don't know it, but hell, the whole church knows it."
Sharon laughed. Seriously, I think you've got a winner this time
and he even loves kids. That jackass you married only loved
himself. Don't you think it's about time you stopped flying solo.
You've both been duped but here's a chance for new beginnings.
Now let's get you dressed."

"Jolene, I'm afraid." It was a simple statement, said in a whisper.

"Relax honey, it's only dinner."

The restaurant hadn't quite filled with patrons when they arrived. Tables were simply decorated with old lanterns in the center. They could easily spot diners as they looked around. A jazz combo was playing softy Luther Vandross's old ballad, "A house is not a home. " They approached the table and the men stood. Zander came to pull out their seats. He was wearing a soft gray leather jacket, blue open-neck shirt and gray matching slacks. Sharon could feel her heat rising. She quickly began drinking from the glass of ice water. They enjoyed a wonderful meal and told tidbits about themselves over wine. She surprised herself and accepted an invitation from Zander to accompany him to the movies on Friday night.

Chapter 6

The pianist promptly started playing at 11:00 a.m. Sunday morning. Pastor Jones led the processional into the Zion Baptist Church, down the center isle into the pulpit adorned with floral pots filled with lilies, signifying the beginning of the Founders Day festivities.

The ushers quickly passed out the programs while the choir led the congregation singing, "We have come into this house, to worship him, Jesus Christ our Lord." Pastor Jones looked out on the membership and guests as they swayed from side to side with hands entwined, held high in the air. Tears rolled down his face as joy swelled in his heart at the sight of many families with four generations worshipping together.

The youth came down the aisles twirling ribbons as they danced to the music. Yellow, red, white, blue, green and black ribbons signifying the colors of faith going up, down and around in syncopation. It was simply beautiful.

Pastor Jones stood in the pulpit and welcomed all present. "This is the day that the Lord has made, let us rejoice and be glad in him." His voice bellowed out for all to hear. "I welcome you to our sixty-fifth Founders Day celebration. Your presence today is a testimony of how this church has served the community and your families throughout the decades. I am honored to be a part of such a significate milestone in this community." He recognized all of the committee chairpersons and congratulated them on a job well done. "My sermon this morning is on, 'Look where He brought us from.'"

As the members and guest were dismissed, they were offered guided tours of the church, followed by an invitation to partake in the luncheon that had been prepared in the Social Hall that boasted some of the best cuisine in town.

SERVICE BROTHAHS
by Doris M. Phelps

The MacArthur High School Marching Band was playing "Yankee Doodle Dandy" as they turned the corner onto Main Street. The bright sunshine beamed off their bright red and white uniforms that had recently been donated by Macy's Department Store.

This year's Memorial Day celebration was the largest the City of Concord had ever experienced. The new mayor, Winslow Mann, and his staff had truly outdone themselves. Mr. Mann was leading the parade in an old 1940 Chevy accompanied by his family. They were followed by an antique wagon pulling a canon, five World War II veterans on a horse-drawn hay wagon, service men from the Vietnam war and fifty proud servicemen who had recently returned home from duty in Iran, Iraq and Afghanistan.

Across the street two disabled veterans sat in a 1999 four-door Ford Taurus drinking from a single bottle of rum. They had watched the parade and all the decorated officers as the day drew to a close. Each man expressed his frustration of the treatment they had received at the local VA hospital, not five miles up the highway.

"Sam, they got a lot a damn nerves acting like all is well, cause we know all ain't right in these here United States where us ole soldiers are concerned," stated John Cooper.

Samuel Ross patted his old friend he considered his brother on the shoulder, "Man, we better get on back home fo this here liquor have us actin crazy and we end up in jail."

John's mother had introduced them, after having met Samuel and instantly falling in love with him. Samuel had never had a visitor in the six months she'd been visiting. "Everybody need somebody, poor chile lying in there day after day suffering and no folks to see about him, well he got us now," she'd declared. As his condition improved she had encouraged John and his father to visit whenever they were at the hospital.

JOHN COOPER

John was nursing a terrible hangover as he struggled to lift his six-foot frame. Slowly he managed to set the table and proceed to the stove to prepare a simple breakfast of eggs, toast and leftover rice. His kitchen was spacious, with large glass doors leading out to the backyard. An island boasting double sinks and cabinets sat in the center. This room was his favorite of all in his home.

He had proposed to Anna here, after they'd shared a banana split and laughed about the concert attendees they had seen earlier that night. "Man, where in the world do people get those getups, they were worse than the Village People with their hardhats, Indian feathers and leather pants," he stated. "You know your folks in the ghetto are known for being in a fashion class of they own. But yo friend in the two-tone wig, platform shoes, and loud-colored plaid bell bottom pants was a sho nuff hot mess." Anna was bent over with laughter.

He neglected the ringing telephone as thoughts of yesteryears surfaced to the forefront of his mind. He'd had a wonderful childhood with two brothers and one sister, now all gone, as well as his parents.

At nineteen he had received papers that the U.S. military was drafting him. He was proud to serve his country, just like his father before him. Three years of trampling through the jungles of Vietnam validated for him that it was a senseless war, culminated by too much death and despair. Hundreds of young men reported missing in action, while thousands lost their lives, limbs and minds for a cause he still didn't understand. There was no probable cause for what he'd seen, experienced, and had to live through.

Finally awaking from an induced sleep, he opened his eyes to capture the beauty of his mother's smile glaring down on him. Dorothy Cooper had been his number one cheerleader. She was just shy of six feet two, tall for a woman. She wore her hair in a French roll with a diamond-studded hair comb. She walked straight up with pride and was as gentle as could be. She was always concerned about the plight of others and the future of children. Discovering that she had driven to the VA hospital each week and stayed with friends for two months, only returning home on the weekends to attend church and prepare food and laundry for his father, confirmed that she truly was their guardian angel. She informed him that the jeep he was riding in went over a mine and three of his comrades were killed. He had lost his lower right leg and undergone four surgeries.

Working for the Red Cross, she answered phones during the day, visited her son during her breaks and as often as she could, always read to him, laughing and telling hilarious stories of family episodes. Late at night she talked to her husband, updating him on their son's progress. Before retiring to bed she prayed, "Dear Lord, please bless and heal my child. Please don't forget the other men and women recuperating in hospitals around the world, along with their families far and near, and give them hope."

John considered himself lucky in many ways. Anna, his childhood sweetheart, had married him regardless of the medical challenges he endured. Unfortunately, they were never able to have children of their own. Anna pursued a nursing career while he built a successful real estate business. Together they traveled, shared their love for blues and jazz, attended festivals whenever their schedules permitted and attended art exhibits looking for just the right pieces to adorn their walls. At fifty-five Anna had suddenly died, a tragedy resulting from a brain aneurysm. His world was turned upside down: their retirement dreams scattered to the wind.

Over the last fifteen years he spent more time with his ailing siblings and tried to be a source of strength for his nieces and nephews. He was committed to preserving the memory of his parents and the work they did to assist wounded veterans. The stress of it all had sent him on a slow spiral downhill, with alcohol to sooth his grieving heart. He had sacrificed and tried his hardest, but he just wasn't as strong as his parents. He had lost control of himself, hiding booze bottles everywhere, attempting to find comfort and a means to numb the pain.

Two years ago his sassy niece Cindy, whom he loved like a daughter, had resigned from her executive position with Proctor

& Gamble to take over his business. Depression and alcoholism were claiming his soul. Facing bankruptcy she stepped in, sold off property, and was able to save his home from foreclosure. Now she managed the office, while he was relentless in fighting for the rights of wounded veterans. Millions were spent on weapons of war, while medical services for those men and women who courageously fought with honor, were still inadequate.

Yesterday had been a catastrophe; he'd found himself haunted by the nightmares of war after placing flags in the cemetery all day. John had awakened drenched in sweat, and he convinced himself that one little shot would calm his nerves and drown visions of the wounded. Sam, who had accompanied him, had finally convinced him to go home, but not before they were both drunk and had vented about how disgusted they felt concerning the current plight of their fellow veteran brothers.

He'd had a few challenges of his own over the years; when his leg got infected or was so tender he couldn't stand to walk. Then there were times when his fight for a new leg seemed hopeless. Following months of petitions he had spent his own money seeking a specialist and paying for it himself. But he had witnessed unnecessary abuse toward veterans too many times. Appointments were canceled after men and women had traveled miles, with nowhere to spend the night except in their cars or in the lobby. There were rude remarks from staff, a bad diagnosis requiring hospitalization, negligence in the nursing care provided at the hospitals.

His battle to help others shouldn't be hindered by things he could not control. Tomorrow was a new day with better services, therapy, funding for improved facilities, and more dedicated doctors and nurses. Also, he couldn't allow himself to disappoint Cindy again. Sipping his black coffee, his mind was made up; tonight he must attend Alcohol Anonymous and call his mentor. He had come too far to let the demons of war take over his destiny.

SAMUEL ROSS

Rubbing sleep from his eyes, Samuel threw back the patchwork quilt and rose to his feet. Catching the bed post he whispered,

"Don't know why I let that crazy boy talk me into drinking; course it wasn't all his fault, if I'd had my meds to knock out that headache I might of thought with some sense." He brought his hand down over his caramel smooth face, eased his five-foot-eight frame slowly back down on the bed and became consumed with his thoughts.

John and me goes way back. Met his mother first, Ms. Dorothy; she helped to take care of me starting when I was at that hospital. She was an angel in disguise who kept telling me, "Stop blocking yo blessings, boy, Gods got yah." Some days I just couldn't cope with the pain. She'd sit by my bed rubbing my hands, hummin her little song and tellin me, "Trust in the Lord."

My homeboy, Earl Tanner, and I had started this journey together. Weren't many jobs for black men where we come from down in Mississippi, and racism was worse than the blazing summer sun. After graduation I convinced him to go with me to the Army registers office to join up. Yep, for four years we were inseparable, in the same troop looking out for each other. We just hoped for a better life and a chance to see more than cotton fields.

Then one day we's marching up the road in Nam, Earl went to pick fruit off a tree alongside the road. Earl stepped on a IED and it blew up right before my eyes. Next thing I know, I was in the hospital with bandages on my head and eyes, screaming. Doctor told me the story he heard was moments after Earl, a bomb blew up the jeep and the door blew off and like to took my head off. I had been shipped back to the states, no idea I'd had two surgeries and been in a coma.

Ms. Dorothy had contacted Earl's folks for me and they had sent me a nice letter with a copy of his obituary. It was a year later before I was able to go back and visit them. Just didn't feel like home without him.

John was a few years ahead of me, so by the time I wound up in the hospital here he had been home a couple of years and was building a life for himself. He'd gone out walking and took a seat at the bus stop when he read the advertisement for a new housing development. The next day he went up to Merritt College and registered for courses in real estate. "I just couldn't stand being caged up in a crowded office with folks talking about nothing all day," he explained.

Many of us veterans didn't have no where to go and no money by the time we was leaving the hospital. Well, Ms. Dorothy had talked Mr. Randall into buying a couple of old Victorian houses and converting them into bed and breakfasts, is what she called them. She had rules posted in each bedroom, a housekeeper coming by on Thursdays, and a woman who cooked two meals a day. I didn't have no folks and this was sho nuff more than I hoped for. After she and John left, I cried like a baby.

Never forget the day Ms. Dorothy was having trouble balancing her bills. I showed her a system to use and she encouraged me to take up accounting classes. That paper hanging up there is my AA Degree, my pride and joy. Didn't help too much cause I was on sick leave every time I turned around, and getting laid off. John offered me a clerks job; he knew the problems I was having. Sometimes I just couldn't get out of bed for days. Well I made him proud and was never late and always dressed to the nines.

Over the years I spent a lot of time at the VA hospitals being treated for migraines. My housemates had all sort of problems too, from being an amputee, drug addict, alcoholic and mental disorders. Ms. Dorothy was our saving grace. She claimed every U.S citizen deserved the best medical treatment, regardless of their skin color and financial status. She always made sure we had our papers in order and questions for the doctors when we had appointments. Some of them doctors and nurses could be downright nasty acting. Had a doctor tell me once, "You just trying to cheat the government, you're pathetic," then called the security when I threatened to knock his teeth out. Ms. Dorothy was so taken aback she got a teacher friend of hers to help us write letters to the mayor, congressman, governor and even Washington. She threatened to organize a march if thangs didn't get better.

"Racism and hatred are a sickness, passed down from generation to generation," she would say. I'd seen a heap of mean thangs growing up in Mississippi. Just never pictured it would be like this up north.

I moved in with John about ten years ago. I'd been back in the hospital and John wanted his housekeeper to keep an eye on me. "Lil brotha, I best take you home with me for a while," he claimed. I just figured he was lonely up in this big old house. But I loved sitting outside on that porch that wraps around the house like in them old movies. So I moved in the mother-in-law section with my own entrance, kitchen, bath and living room. But most of the time I'm up in the main house with John playing cards, or cooking with that lil gal Rachael Ray.

Wow, I'm glad Ms. Cindy is out of town with her family, cause she'd be mighty upset knowing we went back on our promise to stay sober. Sometimes life throws lemons at yah and being able to cope just ain't easy. Through the years we done seen boys from so many wars and wondered what they lives could have been. They was just like us in the beginning, excited and proud to serve our country. Walking past all those decorated graves just made us mad, a sick feeling inside, knowing it was all cause some crazy folks trying to prove something on the battlefields to make a name for themselves. Ms. Dorothy always said, "Just read yah Bible, it's already been prophesized."

Samuel slowly stood, lifting the picture of John and Ann off his dresser. "You two was something else," he whispered. Oh, there was a time when I come close to getting hitched too. Sherry Dunkins was a real looker, with a coke-bottle figure. A real Christian gal that took your breath away just looking at her. Folks couldn't figure out what she and them other women saw in me. Well, I know they was just jealous of pretty boy Sam. But back then I was having so many dreams haunting me, I plain scared her away. Never let myself get that close to no other woman again.

"Time to get to moving. John ain't never liked eating alone and that coffee's smelling mighty good." Sam laughed, wrapping his robe around his body as he walked barefoot down the carpeted hallway admiring the walls adorned with photos of military fighter jets.

"Morning, got any sweets to go with that coffee?" Sam poured himself a cup, pulled out a chair and sat down.

"You mighty perky this morning, bagels in the refrigerator." John pointed across the room.

"Are you going to be all right, John?"

"Yah, man. Let's get dressed and go down to the office, business as usual."

As the two men walked into the local Veterans' Office, a round of applause broke out with everyone clapping: they chanted in unison, "For he's a jolly good fellow. For he's a jolly good fellow."

Sam stared directly at John. "We all figured it was time you got a little recognition for your hard work on our behalf."

John looked around the room with a smile on his face. "Wow, when did you have time to get all this together? " He whispered between clinched teeth.

"Had a little help from Ms. Nadine. Keep trying to tell you she's a real keeper. You need to step up your game." Sam strolled off, waving and hugging the men gathered.

John watched Nadine as she placed a platter on the table, turned and smiled at him through raised lashes. He had to admire Nadine, because she was a strong woman and quite a professional. When he had observed her at church, she was always willing to help.

Music suddenly blared from massive speakers set up in the corner. People had lined up at food and beverage tables, filling their plates and talking.

"May we have the honoree for the night please join me at the mike," Lonell Adams, the director, bellowed out over the music and laughter, "and will someone please bring him a glass of cider."

John joined him in the center of the room. He accepted the glass handed him and nodded at his old friend Sam.

"John, I'd like to present you with this plaque, it's a token of gratitude, for all the work you do on behalf of your fellow Veteran brothers. We know your momma, Mrs. Cooper, would be proud."

John raised the glass in one hand and the plaque in the other. "Thank you all, and let me toast all of you, for your service to our country."

He headed toward the food table where Nadine stood. She smiled up at him as he extended his arms. "Thanks for all your help."

She went into his embrace, her arms across his strong shoulders. "You're welcome, and you deserve much more for all you do for others."

"Well now, don't tell me you two finally see the light," Sam smiled, approaching the couple.

Pulling back, John stared down at Nadine. "How about dinner this Friday?"

Placing his arm around Nadine, Sam planted a kiss on her cheek. "Sure you trust this here fellow?"

Nadine laughed. "I wouldn't have him any other way."

John chuckled. I guess that told you, buddy."

Sam laughed loudly. "That's what I like. A woman who takes up for her man."

Dorothy L. Poston

I am the Director of the West Oakland Senior Center. Oakland native, with over 20 years of experience of working with seniors. I hold a B.A. in Sociology from Madison University in Gulfport, Mississippi, M.A. in Christian Counseling and a Th.D from Sacramento Theological Seminary and Bible College.

I am a licensed ordained minister, musician and writer/composer. I enjoy personal coaching, working with seniors, networking and teambuilding. My passion is helping people empower themselves to do positive things for others. In addition, I like to travel and I appreciate theater.

EXPLORER JONES EXCAVATION OF MOTHER CAVE
by Dorothy L. Poston

It was 1990, and after 10 years of living in the Happy Retirement Home, Explorer Jones (Walter Mitty-type) had returned to his imaginary Egypt to see the woman, "Mother Cave" of the ancient world. Jones considered it as one of the oldest caves in Egypt, and from the tomb many treasures and historic artifacts were found. Jones was known around the home for identifying people, places and things by subjects and titles he used during his (real) employment years.

So, Jones's desire to return to excavate this cave was beyond scientific - it was sensual. Deep in his slumber, he explored the underground maze which led him to generations of mummies packed in igneous rocks that often produced a fire due to climate sensitivity. Any extraction could result in a volcanic-type interruption. Consequently, the experienced explorer always used wisdom by not disturbing unwanted spheres.

Dressed in appropriate (flannel PJ's) attire for the heat, Jones took a gulp of water from his thermos as he used a flat (bed) sheet to wipe the sweat from his brow. In his heart, he heard the moans of the cave: he was not only professional, Jones was spiritual. Mother Cave had been calling him for years to return home. So he entered the sacred grounds with awe and reverence, to find the ancient walls covered with treasures.

The deeper he explored the cave, the more riches and mummies were found. Moments seemed like eternity. Time stood still. Ideas, concepts and visions exploded in a flash. His heart was beating much too fast! It was too late. He was lost in eternity.

Jones always wanted to transit from this life into eternity during an exploration in Mother Cave. His doctors had warned him of his heart disease and that if he continued his explorations, he could have a cardiac arrest. It was 1:27 am, post-mortem examination completed. Dr. Henry Jones died in his bed of cardiac arrest.

MONSTERS IN MY HEAD
by Dorothy L. Poston

Hi, my name is Madeline Parker and I am twelve years old. At age five, I was diagnosed with a rare eye disease among children. Usually, this disease is found in much older people. However, after my mom took me to a specialist, it became clear that my disease had a name, called *Retinal Vascular Occlusion* and I would need treatment. But, there were other issues going on in my head that caused me to receive another type of assistance. Dr. Ivan Kwan was a child psychiatrist, who explained to me that my schizophrenic disorder was like "Monsters living in my head."

Of course, by the time Mom realized that I needed to go to a psychiatrist and an Ophthalmologist, I was already running into walls and putting, things in the wrong place. At five, I tried to reason with my monster; I would talk to it, telling it to stop making me run into the walls and miss picking up my toys. At first, my mother would yell at me for not picking up all of my toys in the living room. Although, I really thought I did. The problem was I didn't see all of the toys due to my illness, but at that time, we didn't know I had an eye disease. My mother thought I was just lazy and didn't want to pick up all of my toys, and I thought my monster was moving my toys around so I would get in trouble.

Even though we lived near a school, I didn't go to preschool. I stayed with my great aunt, who couldn't see any better than me, at least that is what I thought. Auntie walked on a cane, and when Mom would drop me off at her house, she would always greets us at the door and give me a big hug and one of those big wet kisses on my cheeks. Yak! I loved the hugs, but hated the kisses. My mother would give me a hug at the door and run back to the bus stop to catch the 72 which would take her to work.

Every day, Auntie would tell me one of her stories from the many books she had on her wall- to- wall bookshelves. Auntie's house was like living in a library with a playground. She told me I could read any of her books. That way I would be smart when I grew up. She told me not to focus becoming rich. Get my education and that will give me the kind of wealth money couldn't buy. So, at five, during my playtime, I would pretend I was reading to a classroom full of children. My imagination was so real; I could actually see the children in Auntie's living room.

Most of the children had holes in their eye sockets. I couldn't tell if they were looking at me because their eyeballs were gone. The children were from all over the world, dressed in their native costumes and we would play school for hours. Sometimes Auntie would join my class too, just sitting on the floor and talking to my imaginary friends.

When it was Auntie's time to read, sometimes her book would be upside down. The way I knew that it was upside down was because the pictures would be upside down. It was so funny! I remember telling her that one of her books was upside down. She asked me how I know. I told her it was because the sea was at the top and the blue sky and clouds were at the bottom.

She said, "That was good observation. But anybody could see that. See beyond the normal! Walk on the clouds and think deep in the sea". "That didn't make sense to me. As a matter of fact, much of what she said didn't make sense to me then, but now they do.

I told Auntie what was going on during my chores and playtime at home. It seemed like Auntie had the perfect answer for everything! She told me I would be all right. But first, I should make friends with my monster and have him to help me learn the rooms. So, I did. I would go home and learn more of where my mother kept everything, and then return to Auntie's house to report to her.

My monster helped me too. We would count the toys that I would take out to play with and return them at the end of playtime.

Everyday became more exciting at Auntie's house, and our class and play time grew. There were so many people in our class I couldn't believe it. Auntie knew about my eye problems, she told me that it was important to know that I was always bigger than any monster. No matter how large the monster would get, I was much larger than any monster in my head and to make sure that I would read happy books to keep him happy and be sure not to watch too much TV.

Auntie told me that it was better for me to listen to the radio and make up characters in my head to help me visualize specific things. She told me that no matter what I heard- always visualize monsters as beautiful creatures. Auntie said that the TV didn't allow you to create your own world, so listen to the radio and CDs.

We always had cold cereal and fruit for breakfast, and for lunch, healthy sandwiches with juice. My mother would pick me up before dinner time. So, Auntie and I, and all of our monster friends would dance and dance and dance. More monsters visited me. We would dress up in Auntie's old hats and furs with long necklaces.

The eyeless children loved to dance with us. No one ever cared for them the way we did. Sometimes they would bring books to me to have me to read to them. They didn't care that I couldn't read well. They just wanted my attention, and the worse my eyes got, the more attention they received. But I remembered what Auntie said, "Walk on the clouds and think deep in the sea."

Sometimes, Mother would take me to play with other children. But, nobody wanted to play with me, because if we played catch, I would miss the ball. Sometimes, my eye monster would tell me when to catch the ball, and I did. The sad thing is later I developed a heart monster, and my heart monster would tell me that I couldn't play like the other children.

When I was seven, I was diagnosed with congestive heart failure. Several of the valves to my heart were damaged and I would soon need surgery. Fortunately, we had healthcare coverage. At that age, who understands health coverage? I just knew I met another monster! It seemed like we lived at the hospital. They were always checking this or that. Most of the time, I didn't understand what was going on, I was exhausted! So, I would just lie there in mother's arms, as my mother rested in her monster's arms until the doctors or nurse would call me.

By this time, Mother had a massive heart attack, which meant she had monsters. She worked so hard at the oil refinery. Overworked, underpaid and stressed added more monsters. Even though her monsters were larger than mine, I knew they would not get the best of her. I told her she was bigger than any problem including heart monsters.

As time passed, Auntie's illness grew worse, and so did mine. She stopped taking her medication, and her monsters were taking over. Mother told me, Auntie was admitted to a special hospital, like an amusement park for those with uncontrollable monsters living inside their heads. It was like Disneyland to me, except we didn't have to pay to go see her. Mother showed her I.D. and we walked through a gate similar to the park. There, my Auntie and all her monsters would be playing in their costumes. There were so many people there with their own monsters. This was the happy section and everyone with monsters was welcome at Gladman's Mental Hospital.

Finally, I started school. The school kids were not kind to me like Auntie was. The teachers were stressed out and the children were cruel to me. I wanted to learn like others. The teachers called me slow because I couldn't see to read as fast as others, and the kids called me dumb and stupid for the same reasons. So my monsters became my playmates at school too. Some kids found out that I played with my monsters. So, they said I was crazy. After school, they threw rocks and other things at me.

But I remembered to walk "light on clouds and think deep in the sea." I was larger than their monsters. They didn't even know they had monsters too. Time has passed, and now I am twelve years old and I have more monsters in my head. Now, they say it is delusional something. But, it doesn't matter. I feel good about my monsters and better about myself. I get to see my Auntie all the time.

Last Month, Mother packed up all my clothes and brought me to Auntie's amusement park. Now, Auntie and I with all of our monsters live happily in our amusement park. And every day, we walk light on clouds and think deep in the sea.

Mary C. Tate

I was born to Ola Mae and Elliot Sylvester in Whistler, Alabama, the 11th of 12 children. I have been writing since my youth intermittently. I became serious about writing after joining the West Oakland Senior Center's Write-On workshop. In addition to this, I have three children's books in the works for publication and numerous short stories in each edition of the previous publications of our Anthology of Creative Writings by Seniors series.

THE MIGRATION OF THE VAN HOOTENS (WORKING TITLE)
A WORK IN PROGRESS
by Mary C. Tate

CHAPTER 1

April 15, 1849

Dear Cindy,

We have arrived in Springfield where we will soon be leaving with the wagon train. It is only three days since we left St. Louis with all of our belongings, bags, boxes and trunks. I miss you already. We are living in a small barn owned by a black family who kindly took us in as the hotel would not rent rooms to colored people. It is very uncomfortable here. My brothers, Jacob and Josh, love it as they do not have to wash regularly. But Mama, Julia and I are very uncomfortable as you know we were in the habit of bathing daily. The family helping us are very kind and offer whatever they have which is not much. Papa is repaying them by repairing the cabin and barn. That is much needed as they are falling apart. Luckily, since Papa is a master carpenter and wheelwright by trade this place is looking better already. The barn was very drafty so Papa repaired that first and now he is working on the cabin. It is so tedious waiting for our instructions for what we will need to carry on this trip. I know it is a great adventure but I suspect we will have hard times ahead. However, I will not dwell on that. I hope all is well with you. I will write again soon.

Your loving friend,
Rebecca Van Hooten

April 17, 1849

Dear Cindy,
I am distraught! Papa says we may take only three dresses, three dresses! One for church and two for daily wear. He says we must travel light. Poor Mama is crying. She must leave behind her fine china dishes and lace table cloth, both handed down from Grandma Van Hooten, who received them as wedding gifts from the Van Hooten family. Julia is beside herself as she says she is almost seventeen and will be of marriageable age soon but no boy will look at her in drab clothes. Papa just smiled and told us we could take all of our ribbons. We can also take two pairs of shoes but we must exchange our Sunday shoes for another pair of sturdy work shoes. Julia began to wail when she heard this.

Cindy, I miss you and all of my other friends. Papa says there may not be a school, as we are pioneering. This venture sounded so exciting when Papa told us of his dream of moving from the city to a small town in California where he could own his own carpentry shop and build us a nice house on our own land. Mama liked the idea of having her own garden and a few chickens, as she originally came from a small farm. Mama is calling now to get to our chores of sorting out what we may take and leave behind. I will write again soon.

Your loving friend.
Rebecca Van Hooten

April 20, 1849

Dear Cindy,
Things are progressing nicely. Papa was finally able to purchase a canistoga which is a huge wagon covered with canvas. But it was old and rickety. The wheels were bent and the canvas was in shreds. The owner charged Papa much more than it was worth but Papa did not complain. He is fixing it up like new

with Mama's help fitting the canvas. He is adding extra touches for our convenience which I will tell you about later. We will be leaving at the end of the week. Hope all is well with you.

Your loving friend.
Rebecca Van Hooten

April 24, 1849

Dear Cindy,
We are leaving early tomorrow morning. I hastily script this letter to you as Mama says we will not be able to mail another letter until we reach the next town three or four weeks from now. Josh and Jacob are so excited they can't sleep. I hear them whispering and laughing. Julia is in one of her "don't bother me" moods. I am somewhat sad as I realize my old life is over and somewhat apprehensive as to what lies ahead. Mama and Papa are talking quietly and attending to last minute details. I will write as soon as we reach the next town. I hope all is well with you.

Your loving friend.
Rebecca Van Hooten

April 25, 1849

Dear Cindy,
I am up very early to help Mama and Papa. Julia and the boys are still asleep. Papa has done a wonderful job with our wagon. It is painted blue with tall red wheels. The canvas is stretched tight across the top and both ends are pulled in like a bonnet to keep out the sun and rain. Most canistogas do not have a seat in front but Papa put one in for our convenience. There is also a built-in table in back with one leg that lets out for our meals. There is a funny seat on the left side called a lazy seat that a person can sit on to drive the mules. Our wagon has a rounded

bottom so supplies will not shift as we go up and down hills. We are carrying about two hundred pounds of food – staples such as sugar, flour, meal, salt, dried meat, oil, canned peaches, and dried apples. Mama says the fruit is to ward off scurvy, whatever that is. We must also carry supplies such as tools, shovel and axe, extra wagon parts, food for the horses, water for us all, blankets, and rubber sheets for ground cover as I have heard we may have to sleep outside. Papa has made us some make-shift cots that we place over the supplies to sleep on. Most of our supplies are packed in huge barrels and boxes. The spokes that hold up the canvas will be used to hang things on like lanterns and clothing. Each barrel and box is labeled with exactly what is inside so we will not have to search for what we are in need of. I heard Julia and the boys stirring. Now our great adventure begins. Hope all is well with you.

Your loving friend.
Rebecca Van Hooten

May 16, 1849

Dear Cindy,
I am writing to you in the hope of mailing this letter in a few days. The trip thus far has been very uncomfortable. We are so exhausted every night. We must take turns walking a while and riding a while. Julia is so sullen. She is worried about her hair and her skin. And the boys just horse around. It is no fun walking. I just sit and read when it is my turn to ride. I managed to smuggle out some of my favorite books. Mama saw me but pretended not to. So far the trip has not been exciting, just hard work. Julia and I must take turns harnessing and unharnessing the mules, feeding and watering them, and brushing them down. Papa says we must learn every job as we never know when we will be called on to do so out of necessity. Even Mama is learning to drive the canistoga. She grew up on a small farm where she drove a wagon and one horse, but the canistoga is much bigger

and heavier with six mules pulling it. Her hands are aching and swollen at night but she hides that from Papa. The wagon master has placed us at the end of the train as he said the other wagoneers refused to ride behind people of color. Other small incidents have occurred because of our color but Papa says we must take them in stride and think of our goal. It would be nice to have another family of color as company but we are the only ones. At night, after supper, we sit around a camp fire and Papa tells us family history. We have heard it before but now, somehow, it seems more relevant. My turn to take care of the stock so I must end this letter. Hope all is well with you.

Your loving friend.
Rebecca Van Hooten

CHAPTER 2

First Journal Entry
May 22, 1849

Papa says this is what was told to him about his Papa. Papa's grandmother was a woman from Africa. She belonged to a small tribe whose women could select their roles in life, even to become hunters or warriors if they so desired. She was the last of five children, being preceded by four boys. She felt comfortable hunting and fishing, play fighting and wrestling with her father and brothers. At 18 she was young, strong and unmarried. While hunting with her brothers far from home they encountered the slavers who overcame and captured them and took them to the slave ships. She survived the atrosities of the ship, being chained to her brothers, unable to move, lying in sweat, urine, feces, hungry and thirsty, fighting to stay alive. Two brothers did not survive the trip. They talked quietly, trying to give each other courage. Her favorite brother rebelled once too often, was hit several times with the rifle butt. He lay down beside her and never revived. After that, she was separated from her last brother and never saw him again. She survived the middle passage and was taken to a slave auction somewhere in Virginia.

Along with the other slaves, she was washed, greased and given a sort of dress, just a shapeless thing with holes for head and arms. Even in this state, when placed on the auction block, many were struck by her beauty. She was tall, slim and very black. Most of the buyers shied away from her as her eyes blazed with hate, anger and rebellion. They knew she would be trouble. However, one overseer, Perkins was his name, decided to purchase her in spite of a warning that she probably would be trouble. Perkins' boss, Mr. Shaw, was ill and he left the running of the plantation to Perkins. He purchased her and several others and took them away in a cart to some place in Virginia. He gave them names. He decided on her name as Helen. But from the moment she arrived she was rebellious and obstinent. He soon changed her name from Helen to Hellion. He said because she raised so much hell.

One night, soon after he brought her to the plantation, Perkins tried to force himself on her. Then he found out what a warrior she was. Helen had wrestled and tussled long and hard with her brothers. Perkins had approached her without his whip and gun, expecting easy submission, and so was unprepared.

He left unfulfilled with visible bruises and scars of the encounter.

After that, he made her work longer and harder hours in the field and she received fewer rations. Yet, she remained defiant.

Perkins thought to tame her by "marrying" her to a young buck. This young man fell in love with her and treated her gently, staying late in the fields with her and sharing his rations with her. She began to talk to him of freedom and she told him about her life before the plantation. She yearned for freedom. She wanted to run away but did not know this land and where to go to be safe.

She eventually accepted him as her husband. When she found out that she was with child, she swore not to have a child that was born into bondage. She convinced her husband to escape with her. On the night they departed, her husband knicked his foot on a carelessly placed rusty hoe but took no heed of it. By the second day it was swollen and painful and by the third day he could not walk. They were found and returned to the plantation. He was near death and indeed died the next day. Helen was beaten. By some miracle she did not lose the baby. In spite of her pregnancy, Perkins continued to make her life miserable by making her work long hours and giving her sparse rations.

When the baby finally came, he was sickly and weak and not expected to live. That was Papa's Papa. Perkins heard Helen call him Jurii. He thought she was trying to say Jerimiah and that became his name. Helen was fierce about keeping the child by her side, even when working in the fields. He was wrapped in a rag, tied across her stomach so that she could shield him from the sun.

At night, after eating the meager meal she was provided, Helen talked and played with him and sang him little songs. As he got older, in the fire light at night, she would tell him about her home, her brothers, father and mother. She carved little animals for him and told him about the sounds they made which made him laugh and clap. As he got older, he began to imitate his mother and carve animals also. He continued to stay at his mother's side as he was never very robust. Finally, one day when he was about ten years of age, working in the fields with his mother, Perkins sent for Helen alone. Jerimiah never saw her again. That night, he learned that she had been sold away along with several other slaves. He was sent to the kitchen to help. He slept near the wood box at night, and fetched and carried for the kitchen slaves during the day.

Jerimiah talked some times with an old begger who came around to the kitchen asking for food. It was rumored that he had belonged to a prominent family but had been disowned. His name was Mr. Ned. Mr. Ned would sing songs and dance about.

By this time Jerimiah was about sixteen. One day he asked Mr. Ned how it felt to go and come at will and have the freedom to do as you wish. Mr. Ned began to dance and sing a song called "follow the drinking gourd." Mr. Ned looked closely at the boy and said he would visit again soon. After that, he came more often, singing and dancing his way down to the slave quarters and back to the kitchen singing songs. Then one day, Mr. Ned told Jerimiah he had a secret and to meet him at a certain place on the plantation. When the boy arrived, he was surprised to find two other young slaves there like himself. Mr. Ned told them about the underground railroad and that he was a conductor. The three were sworn to secrecy and planned to leave in two days.

At the appointed time, a travelling peddler came by at dusk. He stopped at the kitchen and tried to sell his wares. He was shooed away. Then he went to the meeting place and waited. Soon the three young men appeared and were put into the false floor of the wagon, lying shoulder to shoulder in silence. Jerimiah thought of how his mother described her trip on the ship through the middle passage. They rode for many hours. They were stopped once by the paddy rollers. The peddler tried to sell them his wares saying he had not even sold a thimble all day. He needed money for a meal. They soon departed. Hungry and thirsty, the peddler soon stopped about mid-day in a grove of trees near a cool stream. The young men ate and drank and relieved themselves. They delighted in playing in the water from the stream. They rode again for a few hours more before coming to a small farm. They went immediately to the barn and saw no one. They ate and slept in the barn. The peddler changed horses and when they left again another peddler was driving. They did not exchange names. They were instructed that if they got separated to follow the north star, to travel by night and rest during the day. The strenuous pace began to show on Jerimiah and he was obviously very weak.

They stopped at a prosperous looking farm overnight but when they were about to depart the following morning Jerimiah was still so weak he was told to stay on for a time to gain his strength. Jerimiah was hidden away in the Van Hooten attic. Every morning he looked through the tiny slats of the attic window and watched Mr. Van Hooten groom his favorite horse, a huge appaloosas named Buck. Jerimiah picked up a broken rocker from a discarded chair and idly began to carve a replica on Buck. After about a week, when he was about to leave, he presented Mr. Van Hooten with the carved horse as a thank you. Mr. Van Hooten was so surprised and impressed that he asked Jerimiah if he would consent to stay on for a couple of days. The conductor was against this. It was dangerous to keep slaves in one place for too long. That made the risk of discovery greater. Within the next few days Mr. Van Hooten made a great show, coming back into town with a slave that he claimed he bought from a traveling slave trader who said he was an excellent carver. Also he needed help now as he was getting along in years. Mr. Van Hooten had three sons but they had left long ago for the more lucrative trade of ship building. Mr. Van Hooten wrote out a hasty bill of sale and placed it in his Bible should he ever need it. He fixed a place in his stable. However, each evening he was asked into supper by the Van Hootens. After supper Mr. Van Hooten asked him to stay as he read the Bible each night. Jerimiah began to enjoy this. He especially liked the Christmas story and said he admired the man Joseph. In time, Mr Van Hooten suggested that Jerimiah learn to read and write so he might make deliveries for him. So he taught Jerimiah to read. Mr. Van Hooten already made a very fine living in furniture making, but after Jerimiah began carving on the furniture, business doubled. Every prominent house had a least one piece of furniture featuring some exotic scene such as a lion peering through the tall grass, a giraffe eating from a tall tree, an eland leaping gracefully, or a zebra drinking from a river.

During the day Jerimiah carved furniture and learned to become a master carpenter. He also learned the wheelwright trade. He went about town unhindered and was known as the carver, Mr.

Van Hooten's boy. At night he had dinner with the Van Hootens, learned to play chess and eventually became a formidable opponent. Mrs. Van Hooten served tea and cookies after dinner. She sat and knitted or did some sort of fancy needle work. The Van Hootens came to love him as a son. For Jerimiah, it was the only taste of family life that he had known. In time all thoughts of escaping left him and he took the name of his benefactor. Jerimiah grew to become a fine young man. He could read and write, he had a trade, was well mannered and well spoken. In his early twenties, he desired something more. In his deliveries he covered much of the black communities. He began courting a young lady. He eventually married her. Martha was her name. She was short, plump with a pleasing smile and a kind heart. He built his home on land given to him by the Van Hootens. It was close behind the big house. Mrs. Van Hooten welcomed her. She taught her needle work and sewing. Soon Jeremiah and Martha were the proud parents on a son. Jeremiah named him Joseph. That is our Papa.

Papa grew and as soon as he was old enough began to go to the shop to work with Grandpa Jerimiah and Mr. Van Hooten. When Papa was about 14, Mr. Van Hooten took a tumble from his horse and broke his hip. He never recovered. Papa said he and Grandpa Jerimiah had to take over running the shop. And as Mrs. Van Hooten was elderly and in poor health, Grandma Martha took over caring for them. The Van Hooten boys sent money but never came to see about them. They were satisfied when they heard that their father's slaves were caring for them. Mr. Van Hooten lingered for some months. One day, about six months after the accident, Mr. Van Hooten sent for two lawyers. They closed up in the room for several hours with him. They were both red in the face but were sworn to carry out Mr. Van Hooten's wishes. Several days later they returned with many papers to be signed. Mr. Van Hooten had several neighbors witness the signing. When all the papers were signed and witnessed, Mr. Van Hooten charged the lawyers to keep a copy for his sons, a copy for Mrs. Van Hooten and a copy for Jerimiah. Several months later Mr. Van Hooten passed away. The Van Hooten boys came home immediately but were most disappointed to find that the will was not to be read until the demise of their mother. This occured some months later. The boys came again, already dividing the fortune up in their head. The boys received the big house but Jerimiah's house was not to be touched. He was to be provided ample funds to finish all orders for furniture. When that was completed Jerimiah may sell the house at market rate. The boys complained loudly but all proceedings and transactions were to be handled by the lawyers. The boys did not know that generous funds had been set aside for Jeremiah and his descendents to be issued to him annually for the next 20 years.

CHAPTER 3

June 10, 1849

Dear Cindy,
It has been a while since I wrote. Everything is much the same except we have been hearing shouting and crying in the wagon ahead of us. It is a young, newlywed couple as far as we can surmise. Yesterday the young man shouted at her and threw some of her clothes out of the back of the wagon. Jacob and Joshua were walking behind them. They picked up the clothes and handed them back to her. She smiled and thanked them. We really didn't know what it was all about until the wagon master called a meeting right after dusk. To listen we had to stand on the outside of the crowd as usual. It seems the young lady packed a few food supplies but mostly brought clothes, shoes and hats and not serviceable ones at that. Mr. Payne, the wagon master, said that since it will be about a week before they can purchase rations they will have to eat the evening meal with a different family every night. There was a lot of grumbling. On the fifth day, to our surprise, the couple showed up shyly at our campfire. Mama made them welcome and offered them coffee which they gladly accepted. That night we had corn, okra and

tomatoes cooked with onion and smoked sausage, hot biscuits, sweet hot lemon tea and boiled apples with a pinch of cinnamon and sugar. They ate heartily and gratefully accepted more when offered. The young woman asked us to call her Molly. She was so surprised to find there were no weevels in the biscuits. Molly and Julia talked a bit and seemed to find common ground. The couple came back the next night and the next. The wagon master, Mr. Payne, came and reprimanded them. They replied that they had been to other wagons and they had had enough of half-cooked beans and bread full of weevels. Mr. Payne came to Mama and Papa privately and said if they didn't mind he would take supper with us the next night. That night we had a simple three-bean soup with smoked sausage, cornbread and dried boiled peaches with a pinch of sugar and cinnamon. We drank hot tea but Mr. Payne had coffee. The next night he came by just before supper on the pretense of talking to Papa about his mules. When Mama called us for supper he just stood around until he was invited once again. We all smiled behind our hands. Well, no more news.

Your loving friend,
Rebecca Van Hooten

Journal entry
Our journey continues to be tedious but I grow to admire Papa more and more. Each morning at the break of day he gets up and brings Mama a hot cup of tea. I hear them talking quietly. Then Mama gets up to prepare a hasty breakfast, usually biscuits from the night before and a piece of crunchy salt pork and hot tea. We even get a piece of jerky to munch on until lunch. Mama makes it herself with berries. At lunch Papa supervises the boys taking care of the mules. We have six mules but only four pull at a time on flat ground. Papa rotates the mules so they don't pull every day. Papa says when we reach the mountains we will use all six. All day Papa rides the lead right mule or walks while Mama drives, or sometimes Julia drives. She hates it. At noon the wagon train stops for lunch and to rest the stock. The boys take

care of the mules then. They have to not only feed and water the mules, but check harnesses, hooves, legs and withers. We do the same thing after lunch, that is, walking, riding and fanning dust. We stop about six o'clock for the day. Papa takes care of the team then. He says boys have a little time to play and ladies have a little extra time to do lady things.

There is something else. Papa has rigged us up a little area with a curtain and a chamber pot. He tied a red ribbon on it so when the pot is in use the red ribbon should hang outside. Papa says he cannot have us squatting behind wagons, bushes and trees. At night after all of us have gone to bed Papa takes the pot of waste outside, buries it, and scours the pot with sand as we cannot afford to spare the water. Papa seems to never tire, and he still finds time to joke with us. Papa has a dry sense of humor; he doesn't talk a lot but he says a lot with few words. Mama's hands are tough now and she drives the wagon like a man. Julia continues to complain and be moody, but we are used to it now. The boys are growing up, not so much horsing around. As for me, I dream of soaking in a real tub with sweet-smelling salts just to soak, wash my hair and read undisturbed.

Journal entry
We have six mules. Two we call Tim and Jim. They are big brown mules that look like twins even though they were purchased separately. They are constantly together even when not in harness. The only way we can tell them apart is Tim is a slight bit taller than Jim. Both are sweet-tempered beasts. Then there is Bob who is very strong but seems to be a bit slow witted. Each time we put him in the harness he acts like it is his first time and has to be slapped soundly on the rump to get his attention. He is black. His partner is Ben. They pull well together. The last two are called Tally a who is agreeable, and then there is Mr. Buddy Wicket. Papa named him that. Papa told us that he remembers as a small boy playing in the Van Hooten shop while his Papa worked, when someone mentioned that Mr. Buddy Wicket was on his way, and all gave a loud groan. It seems the real Mr. Buddy

Wicket was a most disagreeable man. He always complained loudly of the cost, and always managed to find something wrong with the work, all imagined, of course. The last mule that was purchased was big, strong and cantankerous. He never wanted to get into harness and would move about to avoid it all the time braying loudly. That's why Papa named him Mr. Buddy Wicket. But we noticed that he never balked with Julia and really seemed to be pleased when she put him in harness. We didn't know why until one day I watched Julia from behind the wagon. She had in her pocket a handfull of grain which she fed to him, and while he chewed he backed easily into the traces.

June 29, 1849

Dear Cindy,
We have left cities and towns behind. Now we occasionlly travel through small communities and settlements. We still cannot find lodging in these places so we just find the nearest river or creek and just camp there. We wash our clothes ourselves. Mama replenishes our water supply but she boils our water thoroughly. Papa goes to whatever mercantile is available. Papa says they will not let him enter the store but when Papa pulls out his list and money, they gladly fill the order and bring it out back for Papa to pick up. While we camp at the rivers there is a lot of wild life about. The boys use their sling shots and we usually have a tasty rabbit stew with biscuits and fresh berry compote for dessert. Julia mentioned it to Molly and she and her husband have started to come with us. You can guess who else showed up at suppertime. Yes, you guessed it. The wagon master came up saying that it was his responsibility to check on all the wagons. Papa offered him supper and he never refuses. That is all our news for now. Hope all is well with you and family.

Your friend
Rebecca Van Hooten

Journal entry

Mama surprised us at the river. She set snares and caught three or four fat rabbits for us to take with us. She skinned them and began to cure the rabbit skins. She said she had a use for them. She also began telling us of her early life. Mama said she never knew a father or mother or for that matter any relatives. Her earliest memory is as a toddler trotting along behind an old woman with many lines in her face and long straight white hair. The old woman did not talk much, but gave grunts and made signs with her hands. They lived in a small shack on the edge of a fair-sized farm. She rarely saw the master and mistress. A few slaves attended the house and garden. The old woman earned her keep by helping with chores. Sometimes they worked in the garden, tended the chickens, fed pigs, and helped take eggs and produce to market. The old woman could have a portion of what was not sold. Occasionally the old lady was called upon to provide a medicine, a poultice or set a broken bone. Mama says the old lady took her to the woods to collect herbs, berries and to set snares. She taught Mama many things by demonstration. Mama did not have a real name until she gave herself one. She heard the name Ola at the market. She liked it and decided to call herself Ola. She loved the month of May with its warm weather and flowers in bloom, so she chose that name too. When she was about 16 the old lady passed away. By now Mama had taken over all the chores the old lady used to do. She was also driving the wagon to market and selling the vegetables, eggs and milk. That is how Papa met her. Mama had to go to market without the old slave who usually accompanied her. Mama was trying to unload and sell her wares at the same time. She was being talked to harshly by a woman who was not accustomed to waiting. Papa quickly went over and helped her unload while she sold her wares. Finally she thanked Papa but would say nothing else. Papa saw her several times in the following months but Papa said she would not even look at him. Mama said she only knew the old slaves on the farm so she did not know she was being admired. Finally Papa decided to court her and he found out where she lived. He thought about talking to her parents for permission to court her. However, he learned from the old slaves that she had no one, and lived on the edge of the farm. Papa went by three or four times before he finally saw her. She usually saw him first and would hide from him. Finally one of the old slaves who looked in on her from time to time sat her down and told her to see Papa. She pointed out to Mama that she had no one to care for her. Papa finally approached the mistress of the farm. The old man was no longer lucid. Papa offered to buy her freedom. The mistress said she had no papers on her. She just came along with the old woman. So when she accepted Papa's proposal she just left. The Van Hootens, Jerimiah and Martha delighted in Joseph and his new wife. They spent long evenings together, Mrs. Van Hooten and Martha and Ola Mae cooking, sewing, talking and laughing. Mr. Van Hooten, Jerimiah and Joseph playing chess, talking and delighting in each others company. Joseph and Ola Mae purchased a modest house nearby. All seemed to go well.

July 15, 1849

Dear Cindy,
We are heading for the great desert. There is less and less foliage, so there is scant wood for fires to prepare our meals. The wagon master called a meeting last night in which he cautioned us to use our water sparingly on ourselves, but give the animals what is needed as they are doing the really hard work. To loose our mules out here in this desolate place would be akin to a death sentence. To make matters worse, now I am a woman. At last. That means extra water for washing for me. I woke early this morning with a bad stomachache and I thought I had wet my cot. But Mama knew immediately what was happening so she took over and now everything is back to normal. And Julia has lost most of her "don't bother me pesky little sister" attitude. The wagon master made a special visit to tell us what we might expect. He dropped in at dinnertime, of course. He told us something special. He said we will have to collect buffalo excrement to use for cooking fuel. He calls it "buffalo chips." He said the dried chips make a nice fire

and the smell is not unpleasant. The boys are looking forward to it. They think it will be great fun. Don't know when I will be able to mail this letter. Hope all is well with you and family.

Your friend,
Rebecca Van Hooten

Journal entry
We are all very sad tonight. Little brother Joey has been bitten by a poisonous serpent. He and Josh were out merrily picking up buffalo chips when it suddenly struck him. He did not even see it. His leg is badly swollen and discolored. Mama quickly cut the leg at the bite site to make it bleed. Then she quickly put together one of her poultices. We are all sitting up tonight. We do not know if he will live or not. Papa is sitting with Mama and praying a lot. Joey moans a lot and he is running a high fever. We are putting cold cloths on his head and Mama is bathing him in some substance. Papa says we must keep up with the train and continue with our chores. The wagon master stopped by to offer his help. All our pots are cold tonight; we have no appetite for food. We are all just sitting and waiting. Julia and I took care of the mules tonight and hurried back to sit with Mama and Papa.

7:00 am–Josh and I took care of the mules this morning. Papa is driving and Mama and Julia are taking care of Joey. I am going shortly to relieve her. Joey's leg is still swollen and discolored.

3:00 pm–There seems to be no change. Mama put on a fresh poultice. She says we must try to keep the fever down and let his body and the poultice do its work. Papa prays a lot.

3:00 am–The fever seems to be breaking. His body does not appear to be as hot as before.

5:00 am–Joey asks for water. Mama gives him small sips.

128 6:30 am–Joey opens his eyes and asks for something to eat.

Mama says he is out of danger. Thank God. Julie came out to help with the mules. Joey's leg is better. Mama says he will probably limp for awhile. Several people have come by with food. We are thankful.

LIFE
by Mary C. Tate

Laughter   Tears

Passing years

Joys   Sorrows

More tomorrows

Smiles   Frowns

Ups   Downs

Then underground

EDUCATING HANNIBAL
by Mary C. Tate

It all started so innocently. He would sit in the window and look out. His aunt had introduced him to some of the neighbors. Ms. Handy lived across the street. He watched her come out of her house, and, as usual, she would stop and check her list just before she got into her car. Sometimes, she would rush back into the house for something she had forgotten. She had left several hours before and when she returned she had four old ladies with her. He watched them for several days from across the street. His aunt had already gone to work, leaving him with a bunch of menial tasks to perform with instructions not to leave the house lest he hook up with his hoodlum buddies. It was almost like being back in prison. Some way for a twenty-two year old man to live, he thought. He wanted to go down to Florida but he had to get some money from somewhere.

There they come again, laughing and helping each other. Mrs. Handy, who he'd named Driver, lived in the house all the time and seemed to be the youngest and spryest. Driver would come out first and start the air-conditioning. Then came Poodle (She always carried a poodle in her arms, like a baby.) Always next to her was Sapphire (he had heard Walker call her that). Walker was rather heavy and always used a walker. And last was Frail. She seemed to be the smallest and oldest of them. That was the lot of them, Driver, Poodle, Sapphire, Walker and Frail. Five little old ladies going out to have fun on a summer afternoon in Houston. Four were visitors, so they had to have traveling money. A plan began to form in his head. How hard could it be to rob five little old ladies?

He continued to make his plans as he sat by the window and watched for them to return. Now let's see. When they get back they probably will be tired and will want to take a nap. That will give me time to scope the place out. Got my duct tape and if I have any problems, I'll get a knife from the kitchen and threaten them. Here they come now. I'll give them a few minutes to take off their shoes and do whatever little old ladies do. He put the duct tape in his back pocket, his shirt hung over it. He crossed the street and rang the doorbell.

The one they call Sapphire came to the door. "Uh, hey lady. My auntie across the street, Edna Perkins, said I should come over and see if I could do some odd jobs for you for some green."
Sapphire didn't say anything. She looked him up and down from head to toe twice, then she spoke. "Young man, I'm sure Mrs. Perkins didn't send you over in this condition. What you are saying is you are looking for a job. Now you need to go back across the street, take a shower, shave, put on clean clothes, wash those sneakers, brush your teeth and comb your hair. Make sure your pants are held up by a belt around your waist, tuck your shirt tail in. When that's done come back and we'll entertain your request." And she shut the door.

She shut the door right in my face. She sounded just like my fifth grade teacher, my ninth and tenth grade teachers too. Damn! He snapped his fingers and went back across the street.

When he returned the next day, he was spit-shined clean, combed and belted. He couldn't conceal the duct tape, so he decided to look for some over there. If he couldn't find any, he could use pantyhose like he saw on television. He rang the doorbell. Sapphire came to the door again. She looked him over very carefully.

"Uh, hey lady."

"Stop right there. 'Uh hey lady' is not a proper greeting. Consider 'good afternoon mam'. My name is blank." And she closed the door.

"Damn! Damn!" he said and snapped his fingers twice. "Well, I gotta do it." He cleared his throat and rang the doorbell again.

"Good afternoon ma'am, my name is Hanny and my aunt across the street, Edna Perkins, said I should come over to see if I could do some odd jobs for a little green, uh scratch, uh cash." And he stood waiting.

Sapphire took his arm and led him in. All the sisters were sitting at the table. "Sisters, this is Hanny. He lives across the street with Mrs. Perkins. He would like to do a few odd jobs for a little cash." Driver spoke up, "Well, we are having lunch now. Have you eaten? We'll set another place for you."

"No thanks ma'am, I ain't hungry" Hanny replied.

"You mean you're not hungry. Sit down." Nobody can resist Sapphire's gumbo. He was seated with a bowl of gumbo in front of him before he knew it. The gumbo looked rich and thick with lots of crab, shrimp and oysters in it over a bed of rice. There was hot French bread and a tall frosted glass of lemonade at his place. He took a small spoonful. He had never tasted anything like this. The stuff Aunt Edna passed off for gumbo was weak, watery and had a few shrimp floating around in it. It looked more like dirty dishwater and tasted like it too.

"Would you like more, Hanny?" Driver asked.
He answered with an enthusiastic "Yes ma'am!"
"Hanny, what kind of a name is Hanny?" Frail was talking.

"Mam, my real name is Hannibal, but that is such a lame name that I just shortened it to Hanny. My aunt Edna said that my mom was into history, but I ain't never heard nothing about no Hannibal, so it's just Hanny."

"Well, young man, I was a journalist and my husband is a history professor. You need to know something about your namesake." Sapphire stepped in. "Don't tell him anything. Let him look it up. But not today. Hannibal, it is time for our nap. So you go home and find out some facts about Hannibal and come back tomorrow."

She took him by the arm and escorted him to the door. "Bye now. See you tomorrow."

He found himself outside the door again. He hadn't gotten past the dining room. "Damn! Damn! Damn!" He snapped his fingers three times and started back across the street.

The next morning as the sisters left on one of their excursions, they saw Hannibal walking down the street toward the neighborhood shopping center. Hannibal passed the nail shop, the ice cream parlor, a wig shop, a small boutique, McDonald's, and ended up at the library. He went in and asked the librarian for books on Hannibal. She directed him to the computer to find the books he needed. Luckily, in the Big Hotel (prison), he had taken a few computer classes and was able to find some books on Hannibal. The librarian asked him for his library card.

"I don't have a library card," he said. The librarian peered at him over thick horn-rimmed glasses.

"No card?!" The librarian said it louder than necessary. Hannibal was embarrassed. "I'll buy one," he mumbled.

"That'll be a dollar fifty, sir" She gave him several huge books. "These are due back in two weeks," she said.

He took the books and walked out. By now the Houston sun was on high. When he got home he was tired, hot and mad. He began chastising himself. What's wrong with me. Those little old ladies are ruining my life. I should have robbed them the first day. Then I would be in Florida now coolin' it. That's it. The last straw. I'm going to do this Hannibal thing, take their money and go. Though he hadn't finished high school he was a fairly good reader. As he opened the first book he noticed the librarian had put in a flyer about getting your GED at classes held at the library. He threw it aside and began to read.

When he looked at the clock again it was about four. He cleaned himself up and went across the street, ready to do what he must. He got in the door without any trouble (he remembered what to say). He was invited into the den. Sapphire and Driver were fixing dinner. Frail and Walker were setting the table. Poodle sat on the sofa watching Law and Order and holding her dog. She looked at him and nodded.

She asked, "How often do you wash your face?"

" Uh, well, Uh mam, your face is not like your hands or your feet. You don't use it for nothin' but eating. So I just wipe my mouth. I ain't real particular about washing." "Washing your face every day, two or three times a day would help you get rid of that acne. You squash those pimples, don't you?" asked Poodle.

"Well yes mam." Hannibal replied.

"Well stop that. You're only making it worse. Wash your face with this soap and stop eating so much fried food." Hannibal looked at her wondering, how did she know I eat McDonald's French fries every day?

Poodle took a pen and pad from the end table, wrote something on it and handed it to Hannibal. "Now you get this soap and this ointment and use them every day."

Just as he was about to respond Sapphire called "Dinner!" and they all went to the dining room and took him along with them. They sat down to a plate of red beans with smoked sausage on a bed of fluffy white rice, a green salad with pineapple chunks and a creamy homemade dressing, a generous hunk of hot cornbread and a tall frosted glass of lemonade. A lemon meringue pie sat in the middle of the table for dessert.

Hannibal dug in; eating so fast, when he looked up everyone was looking at him. Sapphire said, "No one is going to take your food here. We have plenty. Now slow down."

Frail said, "We do like conversation at the table. Now Hannibal, did you find out anything about your namesake?"

"Yes ma'am, I sure did. He was an awesome general. He held the Roman armies at bay for years and occupied Italy for a time. He was a genius strategist and many of his maneuvers are still studied today." He went on to extol the glories of Hannibal. After a while only Hannibal was talking.

After dinner everyone was relaxed. Sapphire and Driver were sitting on the sofa, Frail was reading a magazine, and Poodle and Walker were loading the dishwasher and cleaning the kitchen. Now's my chance, he thought. He casually walked into the kitchen, pretending to help. A set of butcher knives was in a holder on the counter. This is perfect, he thought. Three on the sofa and two in here. Poodle was nearest him, but he didn't consider her a threat. It's now or never, he thought.

He grabbed a butcher knife and said, "I want your money!" Everyone looked at him. The next thing he saw was stars, lots of stars, red, blue, green and yellow stars. When he woke up he was on the sofa. Everyone was looking at him. He wondered how he'd got there. Driver said "Boy, you took your life into your hands. I guess you didn't know you were next to 'Sarge' and she don't take no shit." This time Driver escorted him to the door. "You need to read a bit more about Hannibal. You need to have a plan, a strategy, and know your opponent."

"Yes ma'am," and he slouched back across the street too dejected to say "damn" or even snap his fingers. He watched the ladies leave the following morning.

One year later

Mrs. Handy (or Driver) found this letter in her mailbox.

Dear ladies,
I want to thank you for all your help. I finally realized that robbing people is not the way to get money or get ahead in the world. I took a job at the library and while there I got my GED. I realized that I really like history. I'm now enrolled in the community college and taking a few history classes. I plan to transfer to a four-year institution and pursue a degree. Mrs. Handy has taught me to make lists to help keep myself on track. I hope you are all well. Please accept my deepest apologies for my poor behavior. My Aunt Edna says best wishes and an enthusiastic thank you.

Respectfully, Hannibal

Betty L. Walker

Writing poems and short stories has always been a dream of mine. In Phase 2 of my life, Job 34:14 speaks to me: "I want to stand still and consider the wondrous works of God."

I was born the first child of six to Mr. Eddie, Sr. and Ludy Joe Walker, and was reared in West Oakland, California.

I graduated from Cal State University in Hayward, California and I am active in my church and community.

I hope you enjoy reading my works.

ALL THINGS WILL PASS
by Betty L. Walker

Sunday morning, what a beautiful day. Webster Street Church is full. Ruffled-tier curtains in purple drape the walls. The benches and carpet as well, are in shades of purple. Sparks of light flow from the chandeliers that twinkle like stars from heaven.

People are standing all around me. Sisters and Brothers are dressed in loud bright colors. Louisa Wells has outdone herself today. The red suit she is wearing is definitely designer quality. Rhinestone buttons line the front. Her hat, brilliant red, has matching red rhinestone. She is clapping and smiling to the music. Shouts of hallelujah and praise God can be heard throughout the sanctuary.

Webster Street's mass choir is marching down the aisle, swaying and back stepping, while they sing "Glory to God in the Highest."

A group of men in dark suits lined the left wall. Many of them were singing and raising their hands to the heavens. Deacon Eddie Jones, known to most people as Big Daddy, stood still. It wasn't because he didn't feel the music, his eyes were focused on Louisa Wells.

Big Daddy stood six feet four inches. Daily exercising in the home gym, has him looking younger then his fifty-five years. Tension in his body, and sweat dripping down his back, brings his focus back to the fine sister on row four last seat, in a red suit.

Big Daddy knew Louisa had never been married; she'd taught school for years, and was respected by her co-workers and she was committed. Last year she was named Teacher of the Year. He had often talked to her about church and community matters. Big Daddy wanted to ask her out for dinner to see what could develop between them.

Rev. Mackie and Deacon Willie Lee are the only people in the church who knew about Big Daddy's background. Twenty years ago he spent five years in prison. It was a time in his life when he had lost faith in himself and God. He was divorced, jobless and living with his brother, Eric Jones. One night while sitting in the local bar drinking with Eric and friend, Little Joe, they planned a robbery. They succeeded in getting caught when Little Joe fell and pushed his ski mask off. He told the police their names and all three men were given time in prison. If Sister Louisa knew these facts, would she date him?

Rev. Mackie and Deacon Willie Lee stood up for Big Daddy when he got his city job twenty years ago. Last week his counselor at the local Junior College informed him that he qualified to get his AA degree. He had been taking night classes for three years. He was proud of himself.

Big Daddy was on his treadmill Wednesday when a pain hit him in the side. Oh! I've pulled something, I'd better stop, he thought. It was time to shower and dress for his Men's Meeting at church. He dressed and looked in the mirror. Two gold teeth and a stud in his right ear stared back. His mind kept seeing reflections of Sister Louisa. She was a tall woman, nearly six feet. She weighed close to one hundred seventy-five pounds. She had long big legs, super large breast and a behind waiting to be held. Out the door to the car he went.

Help me Lord! Move my mind back to the road before I have a wreck, he thought The Men's Meeting was brief. Big daddy walked down the hall; the door to Room 10 opened. Sister Louisa and several women walked out of their meeting. Greetings were exchanged. The women split at the door, Sister Louisa, carrying a box of books and a purse, was trying to open the door to the parking lot. Let me help you! I'll carry the box to your car, it's dark outside. Be safe, not sorry. Thank you Deacon. Everything in her car, Sister Louisa smiled and said, How have you been lately? I pulled a muscle today exercising. I like a man who takes care of himself, but don't hurt that body. I need to exercise myself. Big Daddy smiled and said, why don't we set up an exercise and dinner date? I would like that, what Saturday? Pleasantly surprised, Big Daddy said Three too early? No, sounds good. Here is my number and address.

Saturday finally arrived. His hair was cut, he was shaved and showered, and ready to go. He smelled good. Walking light in his new sweats, Big Daddy was unaware of the blue car parked down the street with a stranger watching his house.

Sister Louisa heard the doorbell. Her hands were damp and she was nervous. Dressed in a red sweat suit she opened the door. They were both speechless. Louisa spoke first. Good morning, you look great. Good morning, he said, red is your color, you look beautiful. She grabbed her gym bag and purse and they walked to the car. Down the street, the same car was parked, with a driver wearing dark glasses, watching.

Big Daddy and Louisa arrived at his house. They go in: it looks just like him, neat, clean and masculine. He gives her a tour and they go downstairs to his gym. One large room with a small bathroom. There is a treadmill, free weights, a bicycle and a health rider. I have a bad knee Louisa said. Can you show me how to work out without pain? Put this knee brace on. Let's warm up to this music, and then rotate thirty minutes on each machine. Deacon, I don't know if I can last that long. When you're tired baby, stop. A smile crossed her face, he called me baby.

One hour later Louisa and Big Daddy were huffing and puffing and sucking the air. Baby, stop and drink some water. I need some too. Deacon, I haven't done this much exercising in years. Oh no! I have a cramp in my leg. I can't stand. Big Daddy was up and across the room in a flash. Hold on to me, Louisa, and hop to the chair. It hurts, ouch! Put your arm around my neck and walk slowly. Louisa was leaning on Big Daddy. He felt warm and smelled of sweat and cologne. She could feel the hairs on his arm tickle her arms. Her nipples began to harden, there was slow fire creeping up her spine. She must push away from him before he could tell. It's too late. Big Daddy's manhood was reacting to Louisa's touch. His heart was pounding, he wanted to kiss her red lips. Help me Lord! Do you feel better now, he asked. Yes, thank you. Let's clean up and go upstairs and relax. Louisa got her bag and went into the bathroom. Once inside she stripped, showered and put on fresh clothes. When she came out, Big Daddy wasn't in the room. She headed upstairs and heard water running in the bathroom down the hall. She went into the kitchen and set the table. It was fully set with yellow mums in the vase. The oven was on low. And something smelled good. She took a dishcloth and looked inside. There was chicken browning and bubbling in what smelled like herb sauce. Potatoes were baking in foil. Rolls were set on the stove and a teapot whistled low. A large pitcher of iced tea with mint and lemon floating was on the counter. He had created a marvelous atmosphere. Everything all right? I didn't hear you walk in. The food smells good, the table is lovely, and yellow mums are my favorite. You are something special. Louisa stood up and walked over and softly kissed Big Daddy on the cheek. What was that for, Louisa? Just because, Deacon. He put his hands in his pocket to keep from grabbing her. I don't want to scare her.

Dinner was delicious. Thank you, Deacon. Louisa, let's go to the den and have tea and cake. You have cake too? Yes. Don't tell me you baked it! No! Sister Carrie Brown made it. What did you tell her? I told her I had a date with you. She said she wouldn't tell a soul. No wonder she was smiling at me Wednesday at the Women's Meeting. They both laughed. Her cakes are the best in church. How is your leg now? Feels better, but a little sore.

I had such a good afternoon. It's time for me to go home. They got up and walked to the door. Big Daddy picked up the keys and turned to Louisa. Sister, can a brother kiss you? She looked into his green eyes and felt those large brown hands pull her up against his chest. His lips began to nibble on hers and her arms went around his neck. His kiss started to draw her strength away, and her knees went weak. He felt her and held her tighter. His mind was melting from the heat between them. Deacon, she called slowly, don't talk, just love me back. He felt himself relax, and flow into their passion. Big Daddy slowly pulled back, I better get you home. They walked out of the house and got in the car.

The blue car behind them smelled like smoke and stale food, and musky. Damn, what were they doing all that time? I got to pee. I'm going back to my motel.

The music was loud and fast; it was Men's Day at Webster Street Church. There were at least fifty men in the choir dressed in black suits, white shirts and matching African print ties. The ushers were all male and dressed like the choir. Sister Louisa and several other women remarked how well the brothers looked. Sister Carrie Brown said, my, the Brothers are beautiful today, makes a Sister want to run and shout. The Sisters all laughed and gave each other high fives. Up in the balcony in dark glasses, the man watched. He had purchased a suit and shirt from Goodwill store yesterday. It was amazing what some ironing and spray starch could do. He clapped and rocked like everyone else. The church service reminded him of going to church with his mother years ago.

The service was long, and the offering made a red light come on in his head. The stranger thought one hundred dollars per man, about seventy, he counted, plus the dear sweet Sisters: that offering was close to ten thousand dollars. He could be set for months. He decided to leave early. Walking out, he saw a man taking the money into a side room. Out in the parking lot he sat in his car. Forty minutes later the crowd started coming out, the lovebirds included. Big Daddy walked Louisa to her car. She was in navy blue, with a matching hat tipped to the side.

That night Big Daddy heard a knock on the door. He looked out and Eric was standing there. Opening the door Eric greeted him with, what's up big brother? What are you doing here? Been here for a week checking things out.

I was at your church this morning. I saw that pretty lady you been courting all week. Man you got a good setup. How did you find me? Aunt Lou told me you sent her twenty dollars for Mother's Day, I got the address from the card. Man she still thinks you are special nephew. You want something to eat or drink? No. You really into this religious thang? Yes. I am going to Mexico, got a sweet deal working. I could use a couple hundred dollars. No. Do those church folk know your background? You a moneyman? Your church is pretty rich. Why don't we take that money and go to Mexico? Eric, my life is different now. No more stealing, or police. I want you to get out and move on. Eric got up. Brother, I'm leaving tomorrow, think about what I said. I will call you before I leave.

Louisa, this is Deacon Jones, are you busy? No, what's wrong? I need to come over and talk with you, it's important. Come on, I'll be looking for you. Driving to Louisa's Big Daddy's pain returned to his side. It must be stress. I must hurry and tell Louisa about my background. He parked, walked up to the door, which opened immediately. Fear and pain were on his face. Let me talk and I'll leave when I finish.

Louisa was nervous and her throat became dry. Sit down, Louisa. Twenty-five years ago I spent five years in prison. When I was released the Chaplin told me about Rev. Mackie and his program. I moved here, he got me a job and I have been clean over twenty years. Rev. Mackie and Deacon Willie Lee helped me get my house, introduced me to God, and they are my closest friends. Tonight my brother showed up. He was at church this morning, and he has been watching me for a week. He asked me to help him rob the church and run to Mexico. I kicked him out. Big Daddy sat in the chair and began to cry. My counselor at the junior college told me I have earned my AA degree, I can't loose everything.

Louisa sat down, putting Big Daddy's head in her lap. She slowly rubbed his back and prayed. Tears flowed down her face as she rocked him gently.

The telephone rang. It was Rev. Mackie. He wanted Big Daddy to come to church immediately. Big Daddy and Louisa jumped up and rushed out. They arrived at the church as Eric was being led out by Captain John Jennings, a Deacon and a local policeman in their church. The silent alarm was tripped and the beat cop called Pastor and me. We caught him breaking in. He told us to call you. Do you know him? Yea, he is my brother. I told him earlier to leave town. Eric, why? Man that money could have lasted me for months. Sorry man, take him away officer. As a convicted felon Eric was returned to prison.

Big Daddy grabbed his side. Oh my God it hurts. Captain Jennings and Pastor helped Louisa put Big Daddy in the car and headed to the hospital. Several hours later, the doctor came out. We got his appendices out in time. He will be fine in a week. Louisa sat by his bed holding his hand.

Deacon Willie Lee is my best man, Louisa's best friend Birdie is standing with her. Captain Jennings escorted Louisa into the church. She has on the most fantastic red dress I ever saw. Our love is special. The cruise ship is at sea. Louisa walked out of the bathroom with a red negligee on. Tonight our love comes full circle.

Thank you, Lord!

BLACK CHRISTMAS
by Betty L. Walker

Red, black and green; freedom's colors.
Love, peace and joy; words of the season.
Another year has come to an end.
A calamity of 911; the political, social and religious scandals
of 2001 loom on our horizon.
People feeling bewildered, homeless, friendless, jobless
and depressed.
We see them, we know them, they are us.
In need of being lifted up
In need of an anchor
In need of a friend
In need of God!
War, pain, death, no peace in the world.
What is the news?
HABARI GANI?
JESUS IS ALIVE!
Amen, amen, amen.

LUNCH PAIL
by Betty L. Walker

In the small town of Jonesboro, Louisiana, in 1956, four children from Oakland, California, entered Hawk Elementary School. The excitement of our new adventure was overwhelming. We would ride a school bus for the first time with relatives.

My mother had stocked us with new school clothes and school supplies. Before we left for school I had filled Grannie's lamp with oil so we would have extra light to do our homework. My mother called us on my grandparents' new phone to see how the first day had turned out. She told us our new lunch pails were in the mail, along with our lunch money. The school charged 5 cents for a bottle of milk. My grandmother fixed my lunch each day. I loved fried salt pork (bacon), wrapped in one of grandma's soft biscuits with a small amount of fig preserves. She also included a slice of sweet potato pie and a cloth napkin which I returned home and washed for the next day.

It was beginning to rain when Grannie sent me and my cousin Rose to the smokehouse to get two syrup cans. We were shelling peanuts and cooking down blackberries for Sunday pies. On Saturday, Grandpa would take us, me and my sisters and brother, to town to get our package from the post office.

The week went fast. My aunts and uncles had dropped off my brother and sisters at my grandparents' home for the trip to town. We loaded into the back of Papa's truck, my grandma and smaller sister in the cab. The road was bumpy and rocks and dust flew in our faces. Papa told us to hold the side of the truck. Grannie gave us a blanket to cover ourselves. We finally reached the highway; we can put our blanket down now. The weather is cool and the sky is dark, rain may be coming. I hope we make it back to the country without getting wet.

There is the road sign for town: Jonesboro Three Miles. Our excitement was peaking as Papa pulled into the parking space by the post office. He got out and walked into the post office, "I wonder what colors our lunch pails are?" I asked my sisters. "I don't know; I will take any color," they said. My brother stood and said, "What's taking Papa so long?" "There is probably a line," my sister said.

"Here comes Papa, here comes Papa." We all stood up in the back of the truck. Papa came over to us and set the box down in his truck. He took two ropes and tied one on each side. "Don't let the box bounce out when we get to the dirt road." "We won't, we will put the blanket on top of the box and hold it down."

It took us a while to get home. Grandma had to go to the store; Papa had to get a haircut and gas for the truck. Grandma brought us orange sodas and cookies to hold our excitement down. We are finally on the highway headed for the country. There's our sign, Pleasant Grove Community, left turn, we are on the red dirt road. We pull the blanket over our heads and laugh at each other. Here we go!

There's a trail of red dirt behind Papa's truck. He is watching us in his rear mirror and laughing. All three of us are holding the box tightly. Finally we see our house coming up. We passed Aunt Monk's house, my sister Doris is staying with her family of six; she is my mother's youngest sister. Next we passed my uncle's house; he is my mother's older brother. He has nine children and my brother is staying with them. My sister Pearl is staying with my mother's sister next to her, but they live up by the church and they have two girls. If it sounds like a lot of them, it is. My mother is number ten of twelve, second to the last.

I am the tallest: I jump out the back of the truck. Some of my cousins are coming up the road. They saw Papa's truck and they know we went to get the box. My sister and brother had pushed the box up, untied it, and they were pushing it over the side. My cousin came to help me set it down on the ground.

Papa said, "Take it to the porch, you chaps don't need my help." We all caught the rope my mother had tied the box with and drug it up the steps and sat by Papa's chair. (Two chairs and a bench sat on the porch.) "Hurry Papa, bring your knife to cut the ropes," I said. My grandpa walked real slow, smiling, "I am coming, "he said. He stepped up on the porch and pulled out his pocket knife. He called my brother and said, "Come cut the rope." My brother came up the steps with joy; he had never used a knife before. Papa held the end and showed my brother what to do. My cousin yelled, "I got to go to the outhouse, hurry up." Papa looked up and said, "Hold your peace." My brother cut the ropes, Papa helped him open up the brown paper. My mother had it taped, everyone was holding their breath, and finally the box was opened.

My brother pulled the first package out the box, my grandpa's name was on it. He smiled, and started unwrapping it. The box was long but narrow. He took the top off, a new pair of house shoes. He tried them on and they fit, size 13. The next package was Grandma Lou, and she said, Ludy (my mother) shouldn't have sent them anything. She tore it open, and pulled out a white dress. "It's beautiful and I can wear it on meeting Sunday, (First Sunday)." Grandma had tears in her eyes.

An envelope came out next. It was addressed to my Grandma. Our lunch money and a letter for our upkeep was in it. Papa said, "Lou, we didn't need any money, we got plenty of food and we killing a hog next month." He patted Grandma's hand. By now we were weary and there was no package with our names. Grandpa said, "Let me pull the next one out." He put his hand in and out came a small package with Doris's name. Doris ran over to Papa and grabbed the package. Doris was little, with reddish hair and light eyes. Papa said, "That gal's eyes are twinkling." She ripped the paper off. There was a little red pail with ginger bread children all over it. "It's mine, Faye (my cousin she was forever with) and I can put our lunch in it on Monday." Papa pulled out another package; it said "Pearl" (my sister next to me). She walked real slow and took it out of Papa's hand, Thank you, sir." She opened it and Minnie Mouse was on hers. She smiled and laid it on her chest. Papa said, "Two more to go." He put his hand in again and pulled out a package that said, "Joe." Joe, that's my brother's nickname and Mom's maiden name. He grabbed it, ripped the paper off so fast he dropped the box and everyone jumped. "That's really cool JoJo." Lastly Papa was holding the last package we thought. "Well, Betty Walker, this one is yours." "Papa, you open it." I closed my eyes and put my hands over my face. "Okay, here I go", I heard the paper rip and I heard my family say, "OOOOOooooooooooooooooo." It was Betty Boop. Grandma said, "Let's clean up the porch." But, Papa said, "Wait, there's one more package here." He pulled it out and tore it open. There was a bag of candy for each home we stayed in, with a note saying, "Thank you for taking care of my kids." All my cousins jumped up and down. Papa said, "Each bag would go home with us when we were picked up and the mamas would pass it out.

Monday came and we took our lunch pails to school. There was a lot of staring and pushing to see them by the children in our classes. That night my grandparents called me by the fireplace to say goodnight. Grannie said Papa had something to tell me. "Baby, did you enjoy your lunch pail today?" "Yes sir, all the kids wanted to touch it or sit by us at lunch time, some looked sad and they wished they had one." "Well, your Aunt Pink (my great aunt) said you should leave them home and use your syrup cans since most of the kids can't afford them." I sat shocked, looking into the fire. "You don't want your friends and cousins to feel sad, cry and not want to attend school do you?" "No sir," I answered. "Well go get your can and set it up for school. I'll call the others and they will do the same. You can use it at home." Papa lifted my head and hugged me tight. My tears were coming, but I am strong and held them back, I got up and Grannie said, "I already made your lunch, it's in the cooler." I could see tears in her eyes. "Let's turn the lights out and go to bed. Sam (the bus driver) will be there before we know it." I said goodnight and slowly walked to my room. Betty Boop was sitting on my bed. I held her and slowly rubbed her. "I love you and I am taking you home." I got down on the floor and pulled my suitcase out from under the bed. All the things my grandma had given to me and my extra clothes were in it. Grannie left me a bag. I opened it and put my lunch pail inside. I folded it closed and placed it in the suitcase. One tear fell down my face.

I loved my grandparents so much. For the first time since I came, I wanted my mother and I wanted to go home. I heard the curtain and my Grannie stood there. "You need some help?" "No," I said. She walked over and helped me close the grip, as my grandpa called them. She helped me into bed and put the covers over me. She lay next to me and said, "The south is not like California, baby, people are poor, but we love hard. Here, suck on this candy and say your prayers. Papa and I love you. Good night."

MAYA
by Betty L. Walker

They call me Maya!
The force of her words seemed to move mountains.
They called her Maya!

She sang notes with sweet clarity.
"Plenty good room in my father's kingdom."
They called her Maya!

Rooms light up,
when she recited her poems.
They called her Maya!

Tears came to the eyes of her audiences,
when she spoke of the power of love.
They called her Maya!

She had so much pride
it radiated in her hands and the way she held her head
They called her Maya!

Peace was her battle cry
Save the people of the world; restore respect and dignity.
They called her Maya!

She always said no tears in public.
Traveling the world, speaking to leaders, the common people
and children.
They called her Maya!

God gave you a job to do.
Hearing you speak and sing over the years,
Helped me know that we the people can contribute to society
as well.

Earth mother, sister from the homelands, speaker of the word.
Carrier of peace, rest with the angels, go with God.
Choose your seat and sit down.
Farwell Maya.

"MY SISTER, MY FRIEND!"
by Betty L. Walker

Dedicated to: Betty Britton

My Sister, My Sister!
We are bound by our commonness.
In human beings
In the education of children
In esteem building
In our religious beliefs
And most of all, in our friendship.
My Friend, My Friend!
We are united by our womaness.
Our affection for others
Our need to serve
Our intimacy for life
Our sympathetic nature
And above all our comradery as strong black women.
No matter what life gives,
Be strong! Be Brave! Trust God!
My Sister, My Friend!

RAIN
by Betty L. Walker

Blop, Blop
Pitter, Patter
Pure gold to soil.

SITTING
by Betty L. Walker

Sagging to one side, I hold on!

These strips are making me dizzy.

Tag says, "Wash, Line-dry."

Water makes me very heavy and smelly.

I'm turned in all directions; upside down and inside out.

Flies try to buzz me.

Fat cats, skinny bats, babes give me style.

Nothing I hate more than grease,

I like to sit in the sunshine, or on a cool beach.

I am generational.

You can't get away from me.

I rock, I roll, and stroll.

Many call me classy, others say I am sassy.

By the way, I have many names:

Cap

Sombrero

Beanie

Beret

Stetson

Hat

Kufi

The next time your head needs shelter, call me!

I am available.

SUN
by Betty L. Walker

Sneaking out from the clouds
Rises slowly spreading warmth
Slowly goes down
Sky red and gold.

VILLAGE WOMAN
by Betty L. Walker

We left Mother Africa bound and chained
Tears and screams
Headed for a new land, unknown people,
Languages and customs.
Left our babies, mothers, sisters. aunts,
grandmothers and lovers.
Black women with our nappy hair;
Big brown eyes, and baby bearing hips.
God heard our cries, saved many lives,
Brought freedom, peace and love back to our lives.
What is the news?
Good news, good news.
We have survived, reproduced, created a new culture,
Some pain some gain; war not over, save the children,
Save the men, save yourself.
Respect, dignity and class is what we possess.
Let no one take it away. Hold your head up high;
Strut your stride, smile when you feel like crying.
We are the warriors of the race! Black women,
Mother earth.

Juliana Whitten

I always wanted the two things in life that Freud said were important: to work, and to love. Oh, and I wanted to have fun AND make a difference along the way! For work, I can say with pride that I was a Good Teacher. For thirty years in Oakland and Sausalito/Marin City, I taught large groups of bright, vulnerable, cynical, neglected children and teens to respect themselves, one another, me, and literary skills. As to love, I married interracially and we enjoyed a diverse and culturally rich lifestyle in San Francisco and Berkeley. In 1979 I co-founded I-Pride, the nation's second organization dedicated to the support and well-being of interracial families and multi-ethnic individuals. I also raised—well, maybe guided—two sons to be loving, responsible, creative, funny, productive young men who know how to stay out of jail and contribute to the world. After teaching I mentored new teachers in districts throughout the Bay Area. Now, for fun I get to play tennis, travel this beautiful, endangered planet, and help care for my two grand girls in Washington, DC, my other "home." And I continue to work on the basic lesson of life: loving kindness toward myself and others, remembering we are all One.

GREAT FORCES
by Juliana Whitten

When the yawning night
Exhales its billowing dreams
Great forces are humming
In our innocent beds:

The babies awaken to search for
Their warm mother's milk
In the dark soft
Little heat-seeking missiles
Latch hungrily onto rising nipples
Dripping sweet pale blue living milk.

Likewise the lovers turn over and
Pulled from sleep
Rise up on the fierce tides of desire
Finding their wet treasure in the soft
Folds of darkness.

Elsewhere the old ones open their blurry eyes
Alone or together
To the wondrous miracle
Of another coming day
Glad to be alive, to awaken
To seeing the dust motes dancing
In the rising sunlight
Feeling their hesitant way
Into the sweet diminishing hours
Before the soft dark.

ADDICTION TO CRACK
by Juliana Whitten

Who threw me in this river?
I did, didn't I?
Help! Help me!!
For every suck on the pipe
I'm being sucked under
Swirled around,
Crushed by tons of cloudy water
Dragged over slimy rocks
I can't breathe!
I know I'm drowning
Lungs filling with poison
I can't get to the air...
I'm so tired, so weak
I've tried so hard
I hate this life
I hate me
I want to rest now
In the dark
Let me rest.
Have I forgotten how to swim?
Impossible against the force of this powerful current
There's no fighting it
Maybe I can float...
Face down.

GIVE US THIS DAY
by Juliana Whiten

I hold the beauty of this October
Morning cupped in my hands like hot tea
The crystal air around me
Reverberates with birdsong, breakfast smells, and traffic
Clink of neighbor's spoon against dish
I hold my breath listening:
O that singing mocking bird, a musical genius
On the chimney next door
Riffing his improvisations like Thelonius or Miles.
Under my slippered feet on the flagstones
Red and brown maple leaves fade
Curl, shrink and dissolve
While small apples and new butter lettuce
Offer up their autumnal sweetness.
An airplane passes over.
I am alone, but not lonely.
I have all of today and more,
Those gone and those coming
A breeze passes through
As the sun climbs behind the redwood tree.
I hear the boys are up.
I turn to go inside
To begin making breakfast,
Carrying the scent of this earth
The gifts of this particular place and time
Into the house.

FRIEND OR FOE?
by Juliana Whitten

The new neighbor's black cat
Knows me now, comes over
To rub and be rubbed
A handsome fellow, shy but curious
Missing a hefty piece of his left ear tip
Fur sleek and soft as a mink's
Inky and thick with winter's bounty
He weaves and turns
Walking in circles clearly enjoying
The skittish pleasure of the encounter
Then in a flash
He lunges to bite me
I knock him with my elbow
And he recoils with flattened ears
And dilated pupils in his golden eyes
Ready to do vicious battle, I thought,
Or play...?
Why do I presume he's fighting me
When all he did was half-bite my hand
Refusing my clumsy offering of affection,
Or dominance, he might have thought.
Whose language are we speaking?
He could have sunk those razor sharp teeth
Down to the bone
But instead he merely gestured,
Gave me a warning
That he'd had enough of my petting.
I admired the clarity and directness of his message.
And I'd had enough of him.
I can't wait to see him again.

METEOR SHOWER
by Juliana Whitten

I'm tired and cold, ready to fall into bed,
But I'm staying up to go out at midnight
Echoes of my youth, but even then I would
Only be waiting up to go out at 10...
Why would I do this, old as I am?
I ask myself, what in the world am I doing?
But the reason is not in nor of this world,
It's in the stars, the vast dark heavens above us
Which will light up with shooting stars
One after another and another!
WOW! OH WOW! WOWEE!!
Each one as magical as the last
As good or better than DC's fireworks,
So brilliant, so thrilling and glorious!
I still have vivid memories of the last time
Maybe ten long years ago,
Lying on top of our car,
Dazzled by a meteor shower in another August~
Bright flashes whizzing across the sky
And I figure I better do it now
This year, this summer, tonight,
Before I fall into my grave.

Ahhh, yes, we saw it,
Parked in a shadowed valley
In the hills outskirting Livermore
Near a train trestle at 2 am
Gazing at the celestial show overhead, suddenly
WE SAW IT!!
The mother of all meteors!
A big fiery ball at the head
And a tail unbelievably wide and bright
A thick swath of green white and blue light
Arching through the black star-studded sky
Then hanging there for a while before fading away
We yelled and cried out "Oh My God"
Because that's what we actually were seeing.

NEW LOVE ON THE INTERNET
by Juliana Whitten

We are flying in new skies of imagination
Creating together lovely warm currents of feeling
Which lift us up and up into the gauzy silver clouds
of desire and hope
And dip us down and down into rough gray walls of reality
We have a story we're telling
We're singing a song of being alive and in love
Waking in the mornings to dreams.

This cannot work, this can never work,
Yet we continue to imagine it
Because so far, it works.

And now—so soon— it's over, a rough landing,
Smashed and shattered on the rocks of reality.
Not all acorns are meant to become trees.
There's not enough ground for roots, or sunlight.
The story is ended but not quite in time
For nobody to be hurt.

The fall was hard.
Just think if we had let the story go on, and on...
It's so easy and fun to make up a story,
So hard to put on the ending.
Reality is much more complicated and messy,
And interesting.

SLEEPING WITH MY TWO GRAND DAUGHTERS
by Juliana Whitten

They are so beautiful
Long lashes soft on round cheeks
Innocent and peaceful in their sleep
One on each side of me
Curly hair in my face
Legs thrown over me and each other
A cloud of sweet sweat and bath soap
Wraps us in a damp embrace
Me and my snuggle bunnies
This is pure bliss
This is what I asked for...

Pretty soon I can't stand it
The heat is unbearable
The squirming and random whines
Are driving me mad.
I struggle up from the puppy pile
And escape to the guest bedroom
Where I try to get some sleep
Knowing that the baby will probably
Bark and whine for a ba-ba
Waking her sister and me
In the wee hours of the morning
And sure enough, she does,
And I stumble down to the kitchen to prepare it
And then, I regret to admit,

I forgot to change her diaper
(I am so out of practice with night routines)
And by morning, my lovely bed
with its designer sheets
is soaked in a wide-radius puddle
down to the mattress...
and my lovely girls awake
to smelly tangled soggy sheets,
another bubble bath,
and more love and happiness.
Grandma is exhausted,
And against her best principles
Puts a movie on the television
While she makes breakfast,
Picks up toys, wipes up messes,
Changes another dirty diaper,
And starts the big pile of laundry.
Be careful what you ask for.

THE RIFT
by Juliana Whitten

Setting:	Outside Chez Panisse Restaurant in Berkeley, CA, around 9 pm.
Characters:	John and Kimberly Davis, a white middle-class couple Mary, a black homeless mentally ill woman Sondra, a black homeless addicted woman Ronald, and Donald, black homeless friends of Sondra
Scene:	John and Kimberly are leaving the restaurant; Mary is sitting on the sidewalk nearby.

Kim: Ohhh, that rack of lamb was just exquisite! So juicy and tender! Thanks, honey, for my lavish birthday dinner. I'm going to try making that goat cheese and beet salad next weekend when we have your new CEO over for dinner.

John: You are welcome, sweetheart. You deserve it the way you've been working so hard at your school. You really needed a little R and R.

Kim: Why, have I been crabby lately, honey?

John: No no, I just know you've taken a lot of crap from those kids and that dingbat mother of that little heathen who threw a book at you, what's his name?

Kim: He's not a heathen, he's just angry.

John: Angry about what?

Kim: Oh, so many things are terrible in his life. His parents aren't around, his sister's been put in foster care, and he's being raised by his grandmother who's really old and tired...

Mary: (in a whining singsong voice) Spare change?

John: Sorry.

Mary: (whining) Spare your leftovers?

John: Get a life.

(John and Kim walk a little farther and Kim pulls John to a stop.)

Kim: Honey, that's not like you! What's the matter?

John: I'm just sick of these goddamn beggars hassling me every time I walk down the street.

Kim: She only asked for change. She looks so haggard, maybe she's really hungry. You didn't need to be so rude!

John: Haggard, oh please, baby. Spare me the bleeding heart bullshit. She looks like she's had a few too many of something, if you ask me.

Kim: Well, I'm going to give her some change anyway.

John: Oh good, honey, go on, help her fuel her addictions.

Kim: It's not my business what she does with it!

John: Don't you know you're killing her when you give her money? If not with drugs and alcohol, then killing her desire to get a job.

Kim: Well, she looks like she's dying anyway. I'm going to give her my leftovers.

John: Give away your birthday leftovers? I thought you said you were going to take them to school tomorrow and brag about them in the teachers' room.

Kim: John, I can give away my leftovers if I want.
(Kim walks back to the homeless woman who refuses to look at her.)

Kim: Umm, excuse me, Ma'm, would you like some salad, garlic mashed potatoes, and rack of lamb? It's still hot, and delicious.
(Mary slowly looks at her, points two fingers at her eyes, and says in a preacher's voice:)

Mary: YOU are going to burn in hell with the everlasting flames of destruction and suffer the blights of the everlasting locusts and droughts. YOU are the primeval source of consternation in the wilderness of the pharaohs...

John: Come on, honey, let's go right now.

Kim: I'm sorry if I offended you. I thought...

Mary: (standing up, arms raised) When the trumpets shall sound your offspring will boil in the torments of the everlasting underworld. Your seed will spill forth to wither and die.

John: KIMBERLY!

172

Kim: Ok, here's a dollar. I'm sorry I upset you.
        (John runs over and snatches Kim's arm and pulls her away.)
John: Come on! Right now!
Mary: Oh ye of little faith, know your end is near and your house
        is aflame.

SCENE 2
Setting: The Davis' living room later that evening

Kim: Why aren't you talking to me?
John: I still can't believe you gave that looney a dollar.
Kim: Honey, we spent $285 dollars on dinner. What's one
        more dollar?
John: It's stupid, that's all.
Kim: OK, it's stupid.
John: No, you're stupid. You give money and these people
        multiply like flies in our neighborhood, begging and
        stealing and urinating in public. We can't even go to
        the store without being hassled 4 or 5 times for "spare
        change." Bob Rosen said he stepped in a pile of shit
        last week when he went out to get his newspaper. He's
        putting up a fence now.
Kim: Maybe he stepped in dog shit.
John: How many dogs do you know who use toilet paper?
Kim: I know we have more than our share of homeless around
        here. You know that old man that's always at the corner
        by Peet's Coffee? When I didn't give to him he followed
        me for a block calling me names.
John: When was that? I'll kick his ass.
Kim: Last week.
        (The doorbell rings)
John: Jesus Christ, it's eleven thirty at night! Who can ....?
        (He opens the door. A different homeless woman loaded
        with plastic bags is standing there.)
John: Yes? (Kim comes out of the bedroom.)
Sondra: Are you the couple that was trying to give Mary your
        leftovers?
John: Do I know you?

Sondra: My name's Sondra. You pass me every time you go to the cheese store. You didn't see me tonight cuz I was in the alley. I heard you bein nice to Mary. I watch out for her at night, see, cause she's kinda crazy...

Kim: Well, come in. Did you want the leftovers?

Sondra: No, I wanted a dry place to sleep. It's starting to rain out there. You seemed like nice people, people who care, so I followed you home.

John: Look, can't you find a dry doorway? There's a lot of them downtown on Shattuck.

Kim: Honey, that's not right. She can sleep right here on the couch. Okay?

John: Not okay. Not okay. We don't know her and how do we know what she...

Kim: She's not going to do anything, ... are you?

Sondra: I'm going to sleep good, that's what I'll do.

John: I'll give you thirty dollars and you can go to a hotel.

Kim: John, that's rude! Come on, honey, it's fine for her to stay here. Just for tonight.
(John angrily leaves the room. Both women sit down on the couch.)

Sondra: Thanks.

Kim: You're welcome. So....where are you from, Sondra?

Sondra: Texas, originally. Tyler, Texas. Is it okay if I put my bags over here on this chair?

Kim: Better not, I just had that chair restored and that's silk...

Sondra: Ok, I'll put them on the table.

Kim: Oh, wait, they look a little wet, they might leave spots. Put them here on the floor.

Sondra: (mutters) You sure are picky.

Kim: What'd you say?

Sondra: I said you sure are pretty.

Kim: Oh, thank you. Thank you very much, Sondra.

Sondra: What'd you say your name was?

Kim: Kimberly. Kimberly Davis. (They sit awkwardly in a long silence.)

Kim: Well, let me get you some blankets and a pillow.
(Kim leaves and Sondra walks around studying the

beautiful art, pottery, and furnishings. She hurries back to the couch as Kim enters with the bedding.)

Kim: Here you are. I think you'll be warm enough with these.

Sondra: Thanks, honey, I sure do appreciate it.

Kim: Well, ...good night then.

Sondra: Good night.

(Kim exits. Sondra walks around the room looking over things, snooping in drawers. She finds a spare house key and drops it in her pocket, then sits down in the silk chair, laughing to herself.)

Scene 3

Setting: Kim and John's bedroom. They are getting ready for bed and still fighting quietly.

John: You've really done it now. What were you thinking?

Kim: Relax, honey. We're doing a good deed!

John: Sure, relax. RELAX? With some homeless woman sneaking around in our house? Oh that's really relaxing to me, Kimberly!

Kim: She's not sneaking around! She's probably asleep already. She looks so tired. Let's just get to sleep ourselves. Tomorrow we can send her on her way.

John: You go to sleep. She probably has AIDS. I feel like going to a hotel.

Kim: No! You can't leave me here alone with her.

John: I can't? Why not? I thought you trusted her! Is Miss Goody Two Shoes scared? Maybe if I go sleep in a hotel, you can invite her into bed with you!

Kim: John, you just stop that this minute! You are really being ridiculous!

John: I can't sleep. I'm going to go take a look and see if she's sleeping.

Kim: Don't you dare spy on her. She deserves some privacy, you know.

John: Yeah. Right.

(He leaves. Kimberly turns over and closes her eyes.)

Scene 4   The living room

(John peeks into the living room. He sees Sondra
lighting a crack pipe.)

John: HEY! What the hell do you think you're doing?
Sondra: What's it look like? I'm smoking crack, honey. Want a
         hit?
John: KIMBERLY! CALL THE POLICE!
Kim: (Hurrying in, tying her bathrobe.) What's wrong?
         What's the matter?
John: This lowlife drug addict is smoking crack right here in
         our house! I'm calling the cops! They'll bust your rusty
         ass, lady!
Kim: Wait a minute, John, that might not be a very smart thing
         to do. What if they come in here and search the house
         and find your marijuana?
Sondra: Weed? You got some weed?
John: None of your goddamn business. Now take your bags,
         you ungrateful bitch, and GET OUT! I SAID GET OUT!
Sondra: You shut the fuck up, motherfucker. I'm gettin tired of
         you.
John: (rushing up on her) Oh yeah?

         (Sondra jumps up and throws a hard punch that
         catches John in the eye. Blood runs down his nose. He
         staggers back and crouches down in pain, holding his
         eye. Kimberly rushes to him. Sondra calmly takes their
         cordless phone receiver and drops it in one of her bags.
         She sits back down and takes another crack rock out
         of her sock and puts it in her pipe. She watches them
         steadily as she lights it and takes a deep drag. John and
         Kimberly stare at her. After a minute passes, Sondra
         pulls out their phone and dials a number.)

Sondra: Hey Ronnie! It's me. No, I'm borrowing a phone. Hold
         on, hey, what's the address here? Never mind. (She goes
         to a pile of mail on the desk and reads the address to her
         friend.) Come on over, baby. I'm at 1505 Henry Street.

176

It's a party! OK? OK. Bye.

John: (starts to stand up) Wait just a minute. You can't have...

Sondra: (jumps up and pulls a knife) I can't do what, sucka?

Kim: Nothing. John, sit down, honey. Don't argue with her. (She pulls him down beside her. He sits heavily, drops his head onto his knees. Sondra puts away her knife)

Sondra: Now where's that weed you got?

Kim: It's in the bedroom.

Sondra: Go get it. (John and Kim both start to get up.) Not you, Jack. Just her.

John: My name's not Jack.

Sondra: Yes it is, you's Jump Back Jack. No, you Jack the Ripper. No, Jack and Jill. One thang for sho' is you ain't no Black Jack. (She howls at her own joke.) Where's your liquor, baby? Maybe you got some Jack Daniels? Ha ha ha ha ...

Kim: (coming back from bedroom) Here's the marijuana.

Sondra: Aw, thanks, honey. Now where's your booze, little lady?

Kim: All we have is wine.

Sondra: That's fine. Is your wine fine, is it fine wine? See, I can rap. (The doorbell rings. Sondra lets in a tall, muscular dark skinned man wearing a running suit and canvas hat.)

Ronald: Damn, baby, it's raining out there. (He sees John and Kim) Oh no, now what you got into? What's goin on?

Sondra: These here folks are havin a party. For us.

Ron: Looks more like a crime scene than a party. What's goin on here?

Kim: Your friend Sondra here is high on drugs. She actually pulled a knife on us. (Sondra is opening a bottle of wine and getting out wine glasses.)

Ron: Sondra, how'd you get in here?

Sondra: These nice white folks is havin a party for us, baby, a party! They invited us! Here, have some wine. This here is what rich folks drink.

Kim: I invited her in so she'd have a place to sleep. I had no idea she was on drugs or would have a weapon! I offered her a bed. I trusted her!

John: And she assaulted me when I asked her to leave. And don't think I don't plan to press charges either.

Ron: Whoa! Slow down, now. Why don't I just take her and leave, and you two forget about calling the police.

John: Are you kidding? I'm calling them the minute you're out the door.

Ron: Well, then, I guess I'm not goin nowhere. (He sits down.) I think I will have a glass of that wine. Thanks, baby. (They all look at each other. Sondra gets down and starts to crawl around on the floor looking for something.)

Kim: What's she doing?

Ron: She's looking for crack.

Kim: But there's no crack there.

Ron: It's what she does when she's high.

Sondra: Must be a few crumbs here somewhere. Here's some! Nope, just....

Kim: John, maybe we should just let them go and not call the police.

Ron: Now that's a smart lady. Otherwise it's lookin like a lonnggg night. And Sondra ain't so sweet when she runs outta drugs and starts tweakin. You know what tweakin means?

John: You're going to do jail time for this, brother.

Ron: I ain't your brother, chump. Don't flatter yourself. You a sorry excuse for a man.

Kim: Come on, John, let's just let them go. We don't have to press any charges if they'll just leave!

John: Kimberly, we have to report this crime or they'll just think they can...

Ron: (helps Sondra to her feet and sits her on the couch.) You know what, baby? I think our friends down at the encampment under the freeway might like to come up here and party with us. Where's the phone? I'll call Buster—he got a cell phone—and he'll tell Sophie and Crazy Horse and Fleabag and Junior and ...

John: Wait! Wait! Don't call! Go ahead. Go. I won't call the cops.

Ron: Now how we gonna trust someone like you? Whatcha think, Sondra? Think we can trust him to keep his word?

Sondra: I think he's a lyin SOB. He thinks he's hot shit, but he ain't nothing but a uptight no-heart lowlife coward. He a liar, Ronnie, don't believe him. I wouldn't trust him with my daddy's false teeth.

Ron: (to John) Whatchu gonna do when we leave?

John: Go to bed.

Ron: Swear to God? You even know who God is?

Kim: I'll promise to God we won't call the cops!

John: Yeah, okay. I won't call. I promise. Now leave.

Sondra: To GOD, promise to God. That way He'll strike you down when you go and break your promise.

John: I promise to God. OK? Will you please leave?

Ron: When I finish my wine.

Sondra: Come on, baby. I gotta go catch up with my dealer, cuz he shut down after 2 am. He got a baby now. (She gathers up her bags and stands at the door, peeking out. Ronnie walks up and looks John in the eye.)

Ron: You promise on your mother's grave?

John: My mother's still alive.

Ron: You lucky, man. But I tell you this: if the cops come looking for me, I'll come looking for you, and you will regret it. I will make your life unlivable. Understand? Unlivable. Got it? And that's a promise. Come on, baby. Let's go.

(Ronnie and Sondra leave. John runs over and locks the door.)

Kim: My God, John. What a nightmare! Thank God they're gone!

John: (sinking down on the couch) Now have you learned your lesson?

Kim: I'm so sorry, honey. I'll never be so foolish again.

John: Me neither. Where's the phone?

Kim: She took it! But John! You promised you wouldn't call!!

John: (pulls out his cellphone) That's all right. (Dials 911) Yes, I'd like to report a home invasion robbery, and an assault. Yes, I'm all right, they're gone. It was two homeless people, one was...

SCENE 5   (living room)

> John and Kimberly are seated on the couch wrapped in a blanket, getting ready to watch a Netflix movie on their TV. Kim has made popcorn and they each have a beer. The phone rings and John answers:

John: Hello? Who? Officer Emory? ....Oh, you've got some information for us? OK great! I'll come by tomorrow..... uh, tonight? Now? OK, I guess. Can't it wait til tomorrow? OK then, come on over.

Kim: He's coming now?

John: Yes, he says it's urgent that he talk to us tonight.

Kim: Well, let's watch the movie until he gets here. I'll bet they've got those homeless people in jail by now. Pretty fast work!

> (They start movie, about a minute goes by. Doorbell rings.) John opens the door and Ronnie shoves his way in, followed by a second black man wearing black sweats and a black hoodie who quickly knocks John backwards and pushes him down on the floor. Kim sits in stunned silence. John starts to get up but Ronnie grabs his shirt and forces him on his back, then leans over him:

Ron: So! You broke your promise to God! And now God's gonna teach you a lesson. You a LIAR. Hear me? God don't like liars, and neither do I. The cops came around the camp asking for me and Sondra....and I'm on probation, man. I can't be goin back to the joint.

John: I didn't call the cops, I....

Ron: Shut up! punk ass bitch! My brother D here wanna talk to you. And you better listen good.
> (Kimberly has crept down beside John and she sits close by him. Donald walks over and stands straddled over John. He looks at Kimberly:

Donald: Move, lady.   (Kim slowly gets up and goes to stand behind the couch.) Sit down. If you try anything I will hurt your husband. (Kim sits.)

(Donald stares down at John for at least a minute. Suddenly Donald gives a huge roar like a lion, lunging at John who flinches, covers his head and yells in fear. Donald has a good laugh, and Ronald joins in.)

Kim   Look, what do you want from us? We'll give you whatever you....

Donald: What do we want? Let's see. Whaddaya think, Ronnie? Some money? Some booze? Some pussy?

John: (trying to get up) You better not touch my wife!

Ronald: Or what, punk? You tellin me what to do? Oh, I'm so scared of you. Whachu gonna do, huh? (Donald takes one finger and slowly pushes John back down to the floor. Kim starts to cry quietly.)

Donald: I aint even sliiiiightly interested in your lil old dried out skinny leg ashy face wife.... But now let's talk about your money. I'm thinkin you might got some big money! That right? HUH?

John   None of your business.

Ronald: Oh but that's where you're wrong, my friend. It IS my business! It's the only thing I want from you, and you, my good friend, are going to give it to me, or you will regret the day you were born. Remember I said if you call the cops I would make your life unlivable. Remember? Do you? And now your worst nightmare is beginning...

John: Yeah. (slowly sitting up)

Ronald: Then now you know I keep my word! You will do exactly as I tell you. Agreed?

John: How much do you want?

Ronald: I want everything in your bank account, ...no, you rich people got more than one account, I want ALL your bank accounts. (Grabs John by the throat.) How many you got?

John: Four. But?? Everything? Then how am I supposed to live?

Ronald: Awww, po' little white boy gotta get out in the streets n hustle? You figure it out, motherfucker. You got safety nets all around you. Now get on the phone and start withdrawing. I'ma be listening. (hands him the phone.)

John: Look, I can't do that! (Both Ron and Don move towards him in threatening postures. Ron grabs John's shirt, Don pulls back his fist and Kim screams, and suddenly, there is the sound of a key opening the front door. Everyone freezes. Sondra peers in, then comes in with a look of shock and confusion on her face. She closes the door, drops her bags.)

Sondra: Whatchu all doin here? What the hell? What's goin on??

John: How did you....?

Kim: I told you I couldn't find the extra key, John, remember? She must have taken it when she was here last time!

Donald: We about to extract some resources, some Ben Franklins, baby, from this here piece of shit excuse for a man. And his ugly little wifey.

Sondra: Now just hold up a minute. She been really nice to me. I come over here to give back her key. And her phone. She was gonna let me, she invited me to sleep in her house... they both....

Ronald Look here, crackhead. They tried to get us busted. Get out the way before I ...

Sondra Before you what, sucka....? (Sondra pulls a gun out of her purse and points it at Ron and Don, then at Kim and John....) (the action freezes, silence falls around them all.)

And now, dear Reader, it is your turn. You get to choose how the play will end. Here are a few possible endings, or perhaps you can think of a different one:

1.   Sondra orders Ron and Don to leave, then puts away her gun, tells John and Kim to let her know if they ever need anything, and quietly leaves.

2.   Ronald wrestles the gun away from Sondra and forces John to go with him to the bank for his money. Ron and Don and John leave, and Kim and Sondra sit down, without speaking, and put their arms around each other.

182

3. Sondra, Ron and Don burst out laughing. They tie up and gag John and Kim, pour some drinks for themselves, put on some music, and start looking around for the weed and for valuables and money.

4. Kim manages to sneak up behind Sondra and hit her in the head, knocking her out with a vase. John grabs the gun and shoots Don and Ron, killing both, then he calls the police.

5. Sondra fires the gun and kills Ron. Don comes over and puts his arms around her and they leave together, talking about good riddance, and how they don't really want John and Kim's money.

6. Sondra orders John and Kim to tie up Don and Ron, and to give her whatever money they have in the house. They produce 10 thousand dollars from a safe, and Sondra happily leaves with it. Don and Ron are sitting and cursing while John calls the police.

*Whichever ending you choose, remember that the divide in America between rich and poor and black and white continues to widen. Not all endings are happy, nor unhappy. Life is not necessarily fair, or is it?....and what does your ending say about that? Who are the heroes, who are the villains in **your** play?*

In Memorium

Leslie Hamet

Angela McClain

Vernice Boone

Jackson Royster

www.ingramcontent.com/pod-product-compliance
Lightning Source LLC
Chambersburg PA
CBHW060103260626
47160CB00005B/1787

9 780692 451403